THE SCENT OF LOVE

Book of Love, Book Five

Meara Platt

ARE YOU SIGNED UP FOR DRAGONBLADE'S BLOG?

You'll get the latest news and information on exclusive giveaways, exclusive excerpts, coming releases, sales, free books, cover reveals and more.

Check out our complete list of authors, too!

No spam, no junk. That's a promise!

Sign Up Here

www.dragonbladepublishing.com

Dearest Reader;

Thank you for your support of a small press. At Dragonblade Publishing, we strive to bring you the highest quality Historical Romance from the some of the best authors in the business. Without your support, there is no 'us', so we sincerely hope you adore these stories and find some new favorite authors along the way.

Happy Reading!

CEO, Dragonblade Publishing

Additional Dragonblade books by Author Meara Platt

The Book of Love Series
The Look of Love
The Touch of Love
The Taste of Love
The Song of Love
The Scent of Love
The Kiss of Love
The Hope of Love

Dark Gardens Series
Garden of Shadows
Garden of Light
Garden of Dragons
Garden of Destiny

The Farthingale Series
If You Wished For Me (A Novella)

★★★ Please visit Dragonblade's website for a full list of books and authors. Sign up for Dragonblade's blog for sneak peeks, interviews, and more: ★★★
www.dragonbladepublishing.com

To Aviva, who fills us all with love

CHAPTER ONE

London, England
May 1820

FINN BRAYDEN HAD only himself to blame for being caught quite spectacularly in Lady Eloise Dayne's flower garden in the midst of her tea party with Belle Farthingale in his arms. She wasn't in his arms precisely, more twisted under his body.

He hadn't been kissing her, either.

Nor had he…there was no polite explanation for what he had been doing.

He and Belle had not even been properly introduced.

Not that a proper introduction would have fixed anything.

"Chipping Way curse," he heard someone mutter as a gathering crowd began to close in around them.

"No, it's that book Violet gave her only this morning," Hortensia Farthingale intoned in her doom-and-gloom, dowager voice that was immediately recognizable. "I knew it would lead to disaster."

Finn growled. "Can you not see? She's having trouble catching her breath. This is no jest. Fetch her sister. Quickly!"

He stared down at Belle, this girl who had accidentally spilled tea down the front of his trousers, setting off this series of innocent events that might end up in her ruin. Of course, no Brayden would ever allow such a thing to happen.

Braydens were honorable.

He—damn it—would not be the cause of Belle Farthingale's fall from grace.

"You seem to be having trouble breathing as well, Finn," someone intoned.

"I'm fine." But he wasn't.

After spilling his tea, and while muttering effusive apologies, Belle had unthinkingly reached out to blot the spill with her handkerchief. That was when her hand accidentally touched him where no gently bred young lady should ever touch a man who was not her husband.

His bollocks were now on fire.

Well, not literally on fire.

Whether it was because of the tea or Belle's touch, he did not know.

Realizing what she'd just done, she'd stopped breathing. Utterly and completely. Restoring air to her lungs was all that mattered to Finn right now. They'd sort the rest out later, assuming there was anything to be sorted out. "Belle, speak to me. Please."

He tried to keep his voice calm, but the blood was pumping hard through his veins, and he found himself anything but in control. To his relief, she finally began to inhale. Well, more of a wheeze. He glanced up at the group gathered around them. "Where is her sister?"

He'd heard sitting up helped when someone was in this sort of distress, so he carefully propped Belle up, allowing her to rest in the circle of his arms. "Take slow breaths. There. Well done. Try to take another. I won't leave you. You'll be all right."

He repeated the words, for he noticed they were having some effect. Her chest was heaving less now, and her erratic heartbeat appeared to be regulating.

"Belle!" Honey Farthingale rushed toward them.

Finn felt a flood of relief. "Your sister wasn't breathing. I didn't know what to do."

"Oh, dear. It happens sometimes. I think she's coming out of it."

Belle must have heard her and responded in a strained, raspy voice. "I am."

Finn wasn't so sure, for she was trembling violently, and her breaths were not all that steady. He caught sight of London's most prolific gossip, Lady Phoebe Withnall, staring at him with her beady eyes. "Why are your pants wet?" Her nose twitched as though she'd caught the scent of scandal.

There was no scandal.

Only the scent of grass and flower blossoms and... Belle smelled nice, too. Sweet and subtle as a lavender flower.

He scowled at the incorrigible snoop. Was she seriously going to ruin Belle when the poor girl was in obvious physical distress?

"Let's take her indoors," Honey said, nudging everyone out of the way. "Belle, everything's going to be all right."

Belle nodded, closing her eyes and resting her head against Finn's shoulder when he lifted her in his arms.

To Finn's relief, she appeared to be over the worst of her attack. Perhaps the sight of her sister had reassured her as nothing else could.

"Put your arms around my neck," Finn said, now carrying her toward Lady Dayne's parlor, but there were too many guests chatting and taking tea, so he changed course and took her into the library where they would have more privacy. "It's quieter here."

Honey had followed them in after shooing everyone else away. "Honestly, must they all gawk?" She shook her head and sighed. "Stay with her a moment, Mr. Brayden. I'll have tea and lemon slices sent in. Belle knows what to do now. I'll see if Lady Dayne has some ginger or honey, too."

"I'm so sorry," Belle whispered, opening her eyes and glancing around when they were once more alone. The library door was open, and there were guests lingering in the hall, but no one dared come in. Honey had a no-nonsense way about her that had the others jumping to obey.

3

"Nothing to be sorry about," he muttered, ignoring the feeling of *rightness* that flowed through him while he still held her in his arms. He supposed he ought to set her down. "Belle, what happened to you?"

He'd heard about people who suffered from breathing distress but had never seen this sort of attack before. Braydens were built like oxen. Big. Powerful. Never sick a day in their lives.

"I'd rather not discuss it. I never meant to *touch* you."

It was poor form to show his amusement, but she had to own the situation was ridiculous. He couldn't help grinning, even though her predicament was no laughing matter. "I know. You only meant to help when the tea spilled. It was a kind impulse. No harm done." Other than his burning bollocks, but those did not bear mentioning.

She emitted a groaning laugh. "I don't even know your name. How do you know mine?"

He sat her on the sofa and settled beside her. "Finn Brayden, at your service."

"You're Finn?" Her eyes seemed to brighten, but he could not be sure. She had pretty eyes. "I've heard about you."

Was that good or bad?

She smiled at him so sweetly; he decided it had to be a good thing. "But how do you know me?" she asked again.

"There is no mistaking a Farthingale. Magical blue eyes. Beautiful in an unsophisticated way, and I mean it as a compliment. Yours is not a cold, studied beauty, just natural and warm." He grinned again. "Plus, Violet pointed you and Honey out to me when you first entered Lady Dayne's parlor. She meant to introduce us, but you disappeared. I met Honey, though. She seems quite nice."

"She is. We're very close." She pursed her lips, drawing his attention to them and reminding him that his mouth had been on hers only moments earlier. He wasn't certain Belle remembered. Had she been aware of anything while in the throes of her attack? It did not matter.

His mouth pressing on her soft lips was not a kiss. He'd only been trying to force air into her lungs.

"Did my sister send you into the garden in search of me?"

"No, I only meant to get away from the crowd in the parlor. Then I saw you bending over one of the flower beds and thought you might have dropped something in it. I wanted to offer my assistance in retrieving it."

"I didn't drop anything. I was trying to catch a ladybug and hold it on my finger." A blush now stained her cheeks.

"A ladybug?" All this chaos because of an insect?

"It is said they bring good fortune. Obviously, not true." She cast him a pained glance. "You surprised me when you came upon me. Your footsteps were silent on the grass. Perhaps I was distracted by the ladybug. In any event, I'm sorry I knocked over your tea. I've ruined your clothes. I'll pay for the damage, of course."

"No payment required. I'll take care of it. I should have made my presence known to you sooner." But he'd been enjoying the sight of her nicely rounded backside and was in no hurry to reveal his presence.

He couldn't explain why.

He didn't usually ogle women.

But there was something about Belle that caught his attention and quickened the beats of his heart as he'd watched her bend and twist. She'd given him an eyeful of her slender shoulders, lush chest, slim waist. Long legs.

Then she'd sensed his presence and suddenly turned to face him.

That's when he'd noticed her sparkling eyes and felt the hot liquid spill down the front of his trousers when she'd knocked over his cup.

He could count a hundred debutantes with blue eyes and blonde hair, but Belle's features captivated him. Her eyes were an ensorcelling blue, swirling and ever-changing, like the waters of the ocean. He could swear there were drops of gold in them, too. They were dangerous eyes, capable of drowning a man in their depths.

Her hair was an incredibly rich, molten gold. Perhaps the flecks of gold he'd noticed in her eyes were merely a reflection of her hair.

Her mouth was slightly too wide and ended in a soft pout at the corners.

He wanted to kiss her.

Not here and now, of course.

Hell, yes. Here and now.

"Why does that little woman with a walking cane keep pacing up and down the hall in front of the library?" Belle asked. "I've seen her before, but we were never introduced. Do you know who she is?"

"Yes. She is Lady Withnall." The little snoop was not going to extort either of them with the threat of ruin. He managed her investments. He'd discharge her as a client if she so much as whispered Belle's name. As though sensing he was glaring at her, the harridan started toward them. "Do not speak to her. Let me do all the talking."

"Why?"

Finn heard the *thuck, thuck, thuck* of Lady Withnall's cane. "No time to explain. Just trust me."

He rose to politely greet the woman as she marched in and plunked herself down on the chair opposite the sofa. "What is it with you Brayden men?"

Finn cleared his throat. "What do you mean?"

Hen's teeth.

He knew exactly what she meant. Hadn't she caught his cousin, Romulus, with his hands up Violet Farthingale's gown? And now Romulus and Violet were married.

In truth, they seemed deliriously happy.

Belle looked as though she was about to have another attack. Since she was Violet's cousin—close cousin—Violet had likely told her everything about that incident. She had to know what was coming next.

Without thinking, Finn resumed his seat and took Belle's hands in both of his.

Hers were small and trembling again.

He refused to look at her magnificent chest but knew it was heaving again. He could hear Belle's soft, gasping breaths. "Belle, it's going to be all right."

"Lady Withnall…" She coughed. "You can't…you can't burden any man with me." She coughed again. "I'm not desirable like Violet."

Finn groaned.

He had been ready to fight, to threaten, even to cajole Lady Withnall into keeping her mouth shut about this incident. But Belle had just ruined it for him. He had to marry her now. Wasn't it obvious?

To his surprise, Lady Withnall looked uncertain. "Don't, Finn. I have no intention of spreading gossip about the two of you."

"Thank you," Belle cast her a brilliant smile in relief. "You are safe, Mr. Brayden."

No, he wasn't.

This lung inflammation capable of sending Belle into paroxysms of labored breathing was known to men of medicine. The Latin term for it was asthma. This illness had not only stolen Belle's breath but damaged her spirit and her sense of self-worth.

She was like a kitten who had been kicked hard.

Repeatedly.

And when had a Brayden ever passed up saving an injured kitten?

Even one who was now glowering at him as she sensed his purpose. "Mr. Brayden, don't you dare."

"The name is Finn." He bent on one knee before her.

She grabbed a cushion off the sofa and hit him over the head with it.

CHAPTER TWO

London, England
August 1820

"I KNOW YOU hoped never to see me again, Mr. Brayden." Belle Farthingale ignored the heightened pounding of her heart as she gazed into the sharp, assessing eyes of Finn Brayden. He set down his quill pen and rose to come around his desk to greet her.

Despite the heat of this particularly unpleasant summer afternoon, he appeared cool and collected, his expression unreadable. "Miss Farthingale, what brings you here?"

She stared up at him, hoping he would not toss her out of his office. He could easily do it, for the man was big and built like a warrior. Why hadn't she noticed this the last time they'd met?

To be precise, the first and only time they'd ever met.

What a disaster that had been.

She wished she could wipe that day from his memory and hers, perhaps start over again. Of course, how could he ever forget their encounter in Lady Dayne's flower garden or the chaos she'd created in the midst of the kindly dowager's tea party?

For the past three months, Finn Brayden had been purposely avoiding her, much as one would avoid a dog with fleas.

Perfectly understandable.

All her fault, of course.

"I'd offer you tea…" He glanced at a side table that held a pot and cups on a silver tray.

"No!" Despite her unease, she managed a laugh. "Safer not to, don't you think?"

She hoped enough time had passed that he'd forgiven her.

He arched an eyebrow and cast her an appealing smile. "Right, better to avoid hot liquids around you. How have you been?"

"In good health, thank you. No more embarrassing attacks." She blushed, recalling the incident of her labored breathing that must have frightened the wits out of him. She suffered these attacks on occasion, and they were never pretty. She remembered falling to her knees, then passing out amid a bed of bluebells. Quite ironic, for her given name was Bluebell. Belle was the pet name used by her family.

She couldn't recall what had happened after falling to her knees.

She never remembered anything when in the throes of one of those episodes.

But she had come around to find herself under Finn Brayden's body, his mouth on hers as he attempted to blow air into her lungs. His hands also happened to be on her chest—innocently—to pump her heart when he feared it had stopped.

A small shudder ran through her. It did not bear reliving. "And may I ask, how you have been, Mr. Brayden?"

His appealing smile returned. "Well enough. No one's hit me over the head since you."

Oh, did he have to bring that up, too? She'd only hit him over the head with a decorative sofa cushion to prevent him from doing the idiotically honorable thing and proposing to her. He meant to save her from ruin.

It wasn't necessary, as it turned out. No scandal had ever developed, as she was certain it would not, once he'd explained the circumstances to one and all.

One might say that by hitting him, she'd saved him from a forced and unwanted marriage.

One might also say she had done him a good turn, and he was now obligated to do one for her.

"What brings you here now?" The glint in his eye revealed he had not forgotten a moment of that spectacularly unfortunate day.

He seemed to be regarding her with amusement. She hoped it meant his irritation had waned. She needed him and did not want him to be avoiding her at every turn. "I've come to ask a favor. I am in dire need of your help."

There, I've asked him.

The worst he can say is no.

"My help?" He folded his arms over his chest, awaiting her explanation.

Why hadn't she noticed how daunting he was before? The man seemed more suited to carrying a sword and shield or wearing armor instead of the fashionable Savile Row clothes he had on. In truth, he looked splendid. The cut of his jacket, the fold of his cravat, everything was perfection. The colors were dark, muted. The superfine of his jacket molded to his shoulders and enhanced their broadness.

"Yes." She spoke the word with confidence, hoping not to start *eeping* like a demented bird, for she was not at all confident. "Honey and I are worried. We don't know where else to turn."

He offered her a chair in his very large, very elegant office overlooking the Thames near the Houses of Parliament. "Miss Farthingale, how may I be of assistance to you and your sister?"

He spoke with surprising courtesy, his voice deep and resonant, showing no trace of impatience or simmering irritation. One might believe he was genuinely concerned about her situation.

Instead of returning to sit behind his desk, he took the chair beside hers, and at the same time, with the mere nod of his head, dismissed the clerk who had escorted her in. For the sake of propriety, his door remained open, so Belle's maid could see them from her chair in the waiting room.

"I won't take up much of your time." She was a little overwhelmed by the man now that they were seated side by side. Finn Brayden was more handsome than she'd realized. His eyes were an alluring mix of smoky gray and forest green. His dark hair framed a ruggedly attractive face. "I'll get right to the point." She licked her lips, finding his nearness quite unsettling. "I think someone is stealing from my father's business."

He arched a dark eyebrow but said nothing.

Feeling even more unsettled by his silence, she cleared her throat and continued. "My sister and I attempted to review the ledgers last week, for we are active in the family perfume shops. But our father caught us and snatched them away. We knew at once something was wrong. He's never hidden the accounts from us before. However, these past few months, he has become quite secretive."

Finn stretched his long legs before him and steepled his fingers under his chin. "And you wish me to have a look at these accounts? Will he allow me to do it?"

Belle shook her head. "I don't think so."

"Then how can I help you? I cannot order him to turn the ledgers over to me."

"I know. But Honey and I have come up with a scheme to get them into your hands."

"A scheme?"

Did he just groan?

"Well, a small deception, really. A necessary one if we are to save the family business. We hear you are brilliant with finances and can spot a fraud immediately. This is why I have come to you. Father keeps the ledgers locked away in his desk at our home in Oxford. We have a lovely house just outside of town. Mother is quite proud of her garden, and we have a splendid, shaded walk down to the stream that runs behind it." She toyed with the strings of her reticule, suddenly wondering if this idea she and her sister had hatched was utterly hare-brained.

"You want me to go to Oxford?" He glanced around at his surroundings, the gesture pointing out the obvious. They were in London. In his impressive office. One had a clear view of the boats sailing along the Thames. Indeed, the scent emanating off the river carried on the wind through his open window.

While the breeze was refreshing, the odor of murky water was not. However, she had a particularly sensitive nose, a necessity for a successful perfume business. The odors probably affected her more than it did others.

"Are you asking me to break into your home and steal the ledgers?"

"Goodness, no. If I'd wanted that, I would have hired a professional cutpurse or another local blackguard. The company books must not leave our father's study. Which is why we hoped you might join us there for the week."

"You are inviting me as a guest?"

She nodded.

"And you think your father won't immediately suspect the reason for my presence?"

"Honey and I gave it considerable thought. We first came up with a business excuse, that a client of yours was interested in purchasing our perfume shops and sent you to negotiate with him. But we dismissed the possibility. He won't ever sell. He'd simply send you away."

"So, you've come up with another excuse?" He shifted his large frame and leaned toward her. "I gather this one is more personal. You are blushing."

"It is quite personal." She nodded again, blaming the tingles suddenly running up and down her spine on the uncomfortable request rather than his extremely good looks. "He would not suspect anything if he believed you were courting me."

He threw back his head and laughed. "Miss Farthingale, we've only met twice now. The first time, I was ready to propose to you. This second time, you are proposing to me. Are the Fates trying to tell us something?"

"No. Please don't jest about it. I only want your help."

His humor—which was gallows humor, at best—faded. "What you want me to do is lie to your father."

If he weren't the size of an ox, she'd wrap her hands around his neck and throttle him. "It would only be a small, harmless twisting of the truth. After all, courtship is the reason I've been sent down to London. My parents hope I'll find myself a husband. And this August heat is the perfect excuse to return to the country for a house party."

"Gad, why do I not like the sound of that?"

She pursed her lips to stem her irritation. "We'll invite a few friends, of course. And some family members. Would you like us to invite your brothers, Joshua and Ronan?"

"And have them spy on me as I pretend to court you?" His eyebrows shot up, and his lips twitched in the hint of a smile. "Hell, no. They'll tattle on me to our mother. She is desperate to see me married, especially now that Romulus has done so well for himself. She tried to foist a cross-eyed duchess off on me just last week and the pigeon-toed daughter of an earl the week before that. I think she just wants me out of the house, even though it is *my* house, and she and my brothers live there as my guests."

She sighed. "I'm trying to be serious."

"So am I."

This was more humiliating than she'd expected. Truly, what had she and Honey been thinking? The man was smart, wealthy, and handsome as sin. And though he was determined to make a jest of his situation, it was obvious he could aim as high as he wished for a bride. Indeed, over the course of this season, she'd seen him dance with a host of beautiful young ladies, including a duke's daughter and several daughters of earls, none of whom had any flaws that she could see.

Countless women swooned over him.

Elegant, sophisticated, and well-connected women.

Who would ever believe he was interested in her?

Not even she believed it. She had argued with Honey over who should be the one to approach him and only agreed to do it because there was a hint of gossip about them still floating in the air.

No scandal, just the pairing of her name with his, although most people would have forgotten the reason by now.

She scrambled to her feet. "Mr. Brayden, I'm so sorry. I see now my request is quite ridiculous, and I do apologize for intruding on your busy schedule."

He rose along with her and took her gloved hand. "Miss Farthingale...Belle, wait."

She blinked. "Why?"

He cast her a heart-melting smile. "If I am to court you, we have some preparatory work to do. How are we to convince your father we are falling in love if we know nothing about each other?"

She felt like a mole just come out of its burrow and staring into the brilliant sun. She blinked once more. He was a dark-haired Apollo, the embodiment of a Greek god.

Warmth spread through her body. "Then, you'll do it?"

He cupped her chin in his hand and drew her gaze to his. "I will admit, I'm intrigued. But I'd also like to set down some terms."

"Anything you wish, Mr. Brayden. Happily, if it is within my power to grant it."

"Anything?"

"Yes, of course. You have no idea how grateful I am to you."

He laughed softly and shook his head. "I gather you are not the negotiator in the family."

She winced. "Is it that obvious? No, I'm the fragrance specialist."

"What is that?"

She felt a momentary disappointment as he released her. But his gaze remained on her, the hot gleam in his eyes making her bones melt. Or was she imaging it? This was simply his look. This is why women swooned over him. He was not paying her any particular notice. "I create the perfumes, soaps, and bath oils we sell in our shops."

"You create them?"

She nodded. "Honey's strength is in making the sales and setting up our distribution. I stay mostly in the back room, experimenting with various fragrances. Fruit, spices, flower blossoms. Oils and essences. I have what my family calls a delicate nose, although they mean it as a compliment. I know what will appeal to the ladies who purchase our scents."

He glanced over her head to gaze at her maid, who had her eyes closed and seemed to have fallen asleep in her chair. "Sit down, Miss Farthingale. Tell me more about this talent of yours."

She took her chair once again and tried to remain calm as he settled back down beside her, the glorious heat of his body wreaking havoc on her senses as he sat so close. Butterflies began to flutter in her belly. "What do you wish to know?"

"What is the scent of my cologne? Can you tell?"

"Yes, this sort of test is quite simple for me." She did not know what it had to do with their temporary courtship, but she obliged him. In truth, she had been drawn to his divine scent the moment she'd first walked in.

Clean. Intoxicating. Refreshing.

She put her nose to his neck. *Oh, this man!* Her lips accidentally grazed the rough skin at his throat where his beard was starting to grow back in after this morning's shave.

Perhaps it was not an accident her lips had strayed.

Her body seemed to respond to him in ways her brain could not control.

This could be a problem.

It would take all of her concentration to keep their courtship strictly business. How long would she have to endure? One week, just until their country house party ended and everyone returned to London? Their pretend romance would be over as soon as he discovered who was stealing from their shops.

Perhaps he would figure it out in a day.

That would be a relief, for he was much too handsome for her liking, and she was in danger of doing something very foolish. She needed to save the family business, not ruin her good name.

She'd escaped scandal at their first meeting.

She had no wish to tempt fate now.

Fortunately, she knew she would be safe with him. Why would he bother to seduce a perfume maker with bad lungs?

His lack of interest in her is what would save her.

"Your cologne," she said, casting him a smile of triumph, "is called Claudius, and it is sold exclusively at Harrington's. I know because it is one of our products. Bergamot and sandalwood. I matched the fragrances myself. We also use bergamot in our soothing oils. It has some excellent healing properties."

He smiled. "I think I'm going to enjoy spending the week with you, Miss Farthingale. You are not the typical London debutante. Perhaps I ought to be worried."

"Worried? Ah, yes. Beware, or I shall steal your heart away." She'd need to be far more beautiful and sophisticated for that to ever happen. "No, Mr. Brayden. I promise you, I will stick to our bargain."

He eased back in his chair and emitted a low, deep chuckle. "I wasn't worried about you, Miss Farthingale."

"You weren't?" Did he mean he was at risk of falling in love with her?

She wished he would take this matter more seriously.

Despite his politeness, she knew he just wanted her to go away. That he'd agreed to help had nothing to do with her. He was intrigued by the financial mystery, just as Honey had suspected he would be.

"Save the supper dance for me at Lord Pottinger's ball tonight. And the first waltz. We may as well start immediately. Let others take notice of my interest in you. It will be much more believable if your father hears of our budding romance from sources other than you. Then he won't be suspicious when I show up as a guest at your country party or be overly concerned if I extend my stay for a day or two. Do you think you can feign falling in love with me?"

"I don't know. I've never been in love before. But I have a book."

"A book?"

Her heart gave a lurch when he smiled at her again in a seductively tender and affectionate way.

"Yes, it is called *The Book of Love*. An apt title, don't you think? It's the one Violet gave me shortly after she married your cousin, Romulus. It's an old book with a faded, red leather binding. Violet thinks it will teach me about love. I haven't read it yet."

"Why not?"

She shrugged. "Fear, I think."

"Of love?"

She fidgeted with the strings of her reticule to calm herself. "I wish to fall in love, just not with the wrong man. It's silly, I know. But I'm worried if I read this book, I'll fall in love with the next man to come along. What if he isn't the one meant for me?"

"Don't you think your heart will know?" His voice was deep and divine and filled with genuine concern.

"How could it? I've never been romantically involved with anyone. How can I know if it is right?"

He cast her a thoughtful glance. "Love is a leap of faith, Miss Farthingale. What if I were to read the book with you? Would that make you feel better? In any event, it is an efficient way for both of us to learn more about each other. Besides, we have to understand about love if our ruse is to work. Doe-eyed panic is not going to convince anyone."

"You're right, of course." She gave a wincing laugh. "Do I look that frightened?"

"No, you look lovely."

Her heart fluttered.

Hot, buttered crumpets!

She'd never received a compliment from a man before, not an eligible bachelor who was staring at her in that seductive, I-want-to-devour-you way. She understood he meant nothing by it. And he'd tossed the compliment so casually, he had to be quite expert at flirting with guileless debutantes in their first bloom.

"Yes, Mr. Brayden. I would appreciate your helping me get through *The Book of Love*. When shall we start?"

"Lord Pottinger's ball will run late. How about we start tomorrow afternoon at this same time? But not at your house, or everyone will quickly realize we are faking the courtship. Not here, either. It would not be proper to have you come by my office every day. My clerks will have their ears to the door, their imaginations running wild and not a scintilla of work getting done."

"There is a lecture series on Greek antiquities at the Royal Academy in Somerset House, not far from here. Honey and I were planning to attend. The talks are from two o'clock to four o'clock each afternoon starting tomorrow. We could meet there, perhaps find a quiet corner in the quadrangle. Honey will cover for us, of course. She'll fill me in on what I ought to have learned at the lecture. But are you able to get away from your office for two hours each day?"

"For you?" He nodded. "Yes. I'll mark you down in my calendar as *Appointment with Lady X.*"

She laughed softly. "It sounds tawdry."

He grinned. "I know. My clerks will be too embarrassed to question me about it. And who else will bother to look at my calendar?"

She rose to leave. "I cannot thank you enough, Mr. Brayden. Shall we shake hands? Isn't this what is usually done when a bargain is struck? Although what you are doing for me is more of a favor. How does one properly acknowledge that?"

He rose along with her. "Close your eyes, Miss Farthingale."

She did and felt the feather-soft touch of his lips to hers. A brief, delicate touch. "I'll see you at Lord Pottinger's ball."

She opened her eyes and put a hand to her lips, for they were suddenly tingling. "You kissed me. Is this how favors are commonly acknowledged?"

"I don't know. A mere handshake did not feel right. However, I want you to know that you may back out of this ruse at any time. Don't ever think you are trapped and must go along with the pretense if it feels uncomfortable. We'll come up with another solution if we must."

She nodded.

He frowned. "Are you all right?"

"Yes, Mr. Brayden. I was just wondering about the proper protocol. Would it be impolite if I kissed you back?"

CHAPTER THREE

INN ARRIVED LATER than planned to Lord Pottinger's ball. It couldn't be helped. There were matters he'd needed to finish before heading home to wash and dress for one of the grandest parties of the summer. Now he was here, and the ballroom was a crush. Where was Belle? He hated to admit it but looked forward to holding her in his arms.

The notion was idiotic.

He hardly knew the girl, but he could not deny his anticipation in seeing her again.

Finding her among the crowd proved not to be as difficult as expected. She was dancing with Lord Walton, a rather pompous acquaintance of his from their days together at Oxford University. The pair twirled right past him.

His heartbeat quickened.

Belle looked beautiful smiling, and her eyes were sparkling, for she was obviously enjoying herself as she danced the quadrille. He watched her dip and skip, her gown of palest pink silk swirling about her ankles as she completed the steps and changed partners.

Finn felt a surge of jealousy.

He wanted to be the one to hold her in his arms.

She looked like an angel, her vibrant hair drawn back and styled in a fashionable chignon. The lustrous mane gleamed amber by candlelight, creating the effect of a halo. But his gaze did not linger on her hair, for the graceful glide and sway of her body drew his eyes.

So beautiful.

Yes, he hated the thought of another man touching her. Especially, Walton, that nodcock. He didn't like the way his hand rested low on Belle's waist.

The girl was too beautiful, too innocent. She needed to be warned about men like Walton, petulant lords who were raised in privilege and disdained those lesser in rank. Such men could not be trusted. Not that his own thoughts were pure, by any means. But Belle would always be safe with him. He'd never hurt her, even if the urge to be with her was strong.

Who could blame him? She was as delicious as a meringue confection. Walton thought so, too. The bounder was eyeing her avidly, the gleam in his eyes, revealing his intentions.

Finn watched the man closely, his hands fisted.

Belle suddenly noticed him standing by the edge of the dance floor and graced him with a private smile. He smiled back, holding her gaze until she was forced to turn away to keep up with the dance steps and not break the perfect square.

Walton noticed him as well.

Finn hoped the cold steel now in his gaze conveyed his message to Walton. *Touch Belle, and I will kill you.*

He was never one for subtlety. It wasn't the Brayden way.

Knowing his message had been received, he eased back and tried to wait patiently for the set to end.

He was tempted to cut in, for Walton wasn't the only one wolfishly eyeing Belle. Each time she changed partners within the square, it meant a new man touched her, ogled her. He wanted to chase them all away.

One might say he was behaving like a possessive arse.

Well, he was.

The sight of Belle did something to him, and he couldn't understand why.

She wasn't purposely trying to do anything to him.

And hadn't he gone out of his way to avoid her these past three months? He shouldn't want to have anything to do with her. Not that the incident at Lady Dayne's tea was in any way her fault. He simply did not like feeling out of control. Perhaps it was that he did not like how deeply Belle affected him.

He approached her as soon as Lord Walton returned her to her family, politely greeting Sophie Farthingale and Belle's crusty, elderly Aunt Hortensia first. The old woman might have been considered pretty if not for the sour prunes look perpetually affixed to her face. While Sophie greeted him warmly, Hortensia arched an eyebrow and cast him a cynical I-know-what-you-want-from-Belle look, as though he was a beast who routinely defiled virgins before heading off to work every morning.

He turned to Belle and claimed her for the waltz. As prearranged, he also asked her for the supper dance and then to escort her to supper.

"Yes, thank you, Mr. Brayden. That would be lovely."

Lord Walton grumbled. "I was going to ask you for the supper dance, Miss Farthingale."

"She has accepted me." Finn stared at the man, silently beating him down until he simply skulked away.

Belle appeared flustered.

Finn held out his arm to her, realizing she wasn't used to men vying for her attention. "Walton's a fortune hunter and a cad. Don't ever trust him."

A pained look sprang into her eyes. "I suspected his purpose the moment he came up to me and began spewing compliments. He wanted me to believe I was desirable. Me? What a lark! No man wants me. I'm damaged goods, aren't I?"

Finn was horrified, never intending his warning about Walton to be taken and twisted into an insult. "No, Belle." He took her in his arms when they reached the dance floor. Other couples were already in position. "You are the prettiest girl here."

"Oh, are you starting the pretense now?" she whispered, looking up at him with an uncertain gaze. Did she believe his compliment was meant to be overheard by the others around them? "Yes, of course you are. It's what we'd planned. What should I do next?"

"Nothing, just be yourself." How was he to convince her she was temptation itself when she sincerely believed she was not? This lack of confidence had taken root early in her life and was now deeply embedded within her.

He'd have to do so something to rid her of those choking vines of doubt. Not here, not now. It was something he would work on during their pretend courtship. "I was talking about Walton's faults. You have none. You are an angel, and any man would be lucky to have you as his wife."

"Mr. Brayden—"

"Call me Finn. Save the formality for when we are back in company."

She looked around the dance floor teeming with couples eager for the waltz to start. "Isn't this company? We're surrounded by ladies and gentlemen who are waiting for the orchestra to strike the first chords."

"No, Belle. You are in my arms. I have you all to myself. No one else matters but you and me. No one else can hear us or cares to. This is why the waltz is considered scandalous, the intimacy it allows couples."

She nodded earnestly, her lips now pursed as she began to fret about a new thing. Perhaps it was the same I'm-not-worthy tune she'd been humming ever since she'd first experienced these attacks. How old was she the first time she'd lost her breath? He wouldn't ask her, for he wanted her to think of him and their dance.

He wanted her to feel beautiful and worthwhile.

She continued to fret. What was it now? His nearness? Her lungs? "Belle, just nod to me if you tire. We don't have to finish the waltz. I'll take you for a turn on the veranda. Or return you to your family, if you prefer."

"The veranda will do. But I'm sure it won't be necessary. I'll make it through the dance."

He wasn't so certain. The room was hot and crowded, the odor of exertion and sweating bodies quite pungent. His nose wasn't nearly as sensitive as Belle's, and he found the scent unpleasant.

Belle would be overwhelmed by it.

As the first notes were struck and they began to move in a whirl with the other dancers, Finn sought to distract her. "What cologne am I wearing this evening?"

He leaned forward, allowing her nose and lips to graze his neck as she breathed him in.

Lord, the sweet, soft touch of her lips.

She shook her head and grinned. "Ah, you've put on a new fragrance. Another of my creations. It's called Pharaoh. Primarily sandalwood with a dash of clove and sea salt tossed in. I also use clove in my bath oils to enhance their healing properties. Clove is good for one's bones and liver and for tooth pain. However, only in small doses. Too much, and it can have toxic effects."

"How do you know so much about plants and their healing properties?"

"I read everything I can find on the topic. I also go to the local spice markets, especially the ones located in port towns where one might meet foreign travelers. My father takes me there, of course. I am never permitted to go on my own."

"Have you gone while in London?"

"Yes, with my Uncle John. He's taken me several times to the London markets and even to the docks. Ships sail in from all over the world, carrying exotic merchandise. You'd be amazed what one can find being unloaded off these vessels. I've learned so much. I'd love to travel to these foreign lands to see where these spices, teas, and fruit are grown. I'd love to know how they feel in my hands and how they smell when freshly picked. Most of what I find in England is dried or turned into powder already. I'd also love to study with renowned healers."

"I had no idea you are quite the scholar."

"Hardly, but my interest started because I was desperate to find a cure for these attacks of breathlessness. That's how I learned about the healing properties of ginger, honey, tea, and lemons. All are helpful, perhaps not in ultimately curing me, but in easing the symptoms when they arise."

"Will you teach me?"

She looked up at him, surprised. "Truly?"

"Yes. I enjoy studying new things. Why do you think I've become successful at what I do?" As they spoke, he slowed his steps and moderated the spins so that they moved like a gently flowing stream rather than a fast-paced current.

He hoped Belle would not notice they were moving slower than the other dancers and take offense.

"You're successful because you understand finances, probably were born knowing everything there is to know on the topic." She laughed lightly. "I can see you as a little boy, trading with your brothers and cousins. *I'll give you two marbles for your slingshot.* The next thing they know, you own three houses, and they're left fighting over your slingshot."

He arched an eyebrow and grinned. "I may have done. I learned early on about the nature of people. It isn't merely having wealth to trade, but how one trades it."

"What do you mean?"

"Everyone views a shilling differently. I may give a shilling to one man, and he will have it spent before it's ever tucked away in his pocket. I can give it to another, and he will tuck it in his pocket and never use it. I can give it to a third man, and he will trade that shilling, build on it until he has made four shillings out of it."

"Finn, this is so interesting. Will you teach me more?"

"Any time, Belle." Something odd happened to him. The world seemed to melt away, leaving only the two of them together amid the soft candlelight and enrapturing music. He had his hand to the small of her back and his other hand clasping hers. She moved easily, gracefully, her body finely attuned to his as he led her through the steps.

Her body.

She felt soft. Warm. Somehow a perfect fit to his large frame.

But more important, he felt comfortable with her and knew he could talk to her for hours without ever growing bored. When had he spoken more than two words to any other young lady while dancing? With other dance partners, it was a strain to find topics of conversation and most of them were dull. A remark about the next ball of consequence to be held in London. A polite comment about the young lady's gown. Or the weather. Or her family.

With Belle, he could pour out his innermost thoughts or easily chat about anything or nothing important at all.

They seemed to be doing well until Belle made a slight misstep. She looked up at him with pleading eyes. "Finn...I'm so sorry. I can't..."

They were near the double doors opening onto the veranda. "Let's go outside."

She nodded.

He led her to a stone bench in full view of the ballroom. She sat and wordlessly stared down at her feet. He could not tell if she was quiet in order to catch her breath or merely disappointed she could not finish the waltz.

She did not seem to be gasping for air.

Nor did she appear to be struggling in any way, except to hold back tears of disappointment.

He remained standing beside her, watching her carefully. With her head down, all he could see was her beautiful mass of molten curls and her slumped shoulders.

The air was heavy, no sign of a breeze, just the oppressive scent of lilacs. He recognized the fragrance, for he had lilac trees in his garden. They flowered in spring, their blooms dying by the beginning of summer. But their leaves held on to the pungent scent throughout the season, and it surrounded them now. Old and stale, like used coffee grinds.

Nor did it help that the night was hot and humid. "I'm not sure if this is any better for you, Belle."

"It is." She clasped her hands tightly together. "I hate this weakness in me. I hate how everyone treats me like a porcelain doll, so fragile and easy to shatter. And yet, they're right. I wanted to make it through the dance so badly."

"Don't be too hard on yourself. You danced the opening set, and I'm sure it lasted almost an hour."

She finally looked up at him. "Most of the time we stood, awaiting our turn."

"In the hot room, amid a crowd. Are you going to kick yourself all night long?"

She frowned at him. "Easy for you to say. You're strong as an ox. Nothing can fell you."

"I'm sure there are plenty of things that can take me down. We all have different strengths and weaknesses."

"You don't. You're perfect."

He liked that she thought so, but he couldn't hold back a laugh. "Ha! Shows how little you know about me. I am far from perfect, just ask my brothers. They'll give you an earful. And why are you comparing yourself to me? You don't know me well enough yet to form an opinion. I've made plenty of mistakes. Life would be deadly dull if we never made them."

"Name one mistake you've made this evening?"

He sank onto the bench beside her. "You start first. Name one you've made."

"How can you ask that? I couldn't finish the dance."

"That is not a mistake, Belle. It is merely a fact. Mistakes have consequences. My kissing you now would be a mistake."

"Because others would see us."

He nodded.

"And you'd be forced to marry me to save me from ruin?" She frowned at him. "Your honorable impulses are most irritating. Let's be clear about the arrangement. You and I are not going to marry. We are just pretending."

"Let me be clear on *my* terms. If you are in trouble, I will marry you to protect you. That is not negotiable."

"How will I be in trouble?" She rolled her eyes. "You're not going to kiss me, so I'm safe there. And what is the worst that can happen if my father catches us going over his ledgers? He's my father, and he loves me. Perhaps he will send you packing and me up to bed without my supper, but that's all."

"No, Belle. The worst that can happen is you getting caught in the middle of dangerous business between your father and some very unsavory characters. Do you think whoever might be stealing from the business is going to surrender quietly if found out? And what if you unwittingly stumble onto something larger than an employee skimming off the profits?"

She opened her mouth to protest, then clamped it shut. "What interest would any shady character have in a perfume shop?"

"Shops," he corrected. "You have more than one, and they're all doing quite well. I don't know yet what your father is hiding. But I don't need to examine the ledgers to know that you are the heart of this successful operation."

"Me?" She looked at him, genuinely confused. "How?"

"Your delicate nose." He shifted beside her, the short hairs on the back of his neck now tingling. Why hadn't he realized it sooner? "Your soaps and perfumes are sold everywhere. The colognes I purchase, Claudius and Pharaoh, are the most popular items stocked at Harrington's. I'll bet odds if I were to ask their manager what the five top sellers are, they'd all be your fragrances."

"Well, I am proud of what I do."

"As you ought to be. Your business thrives because of you. Honey can make those sales because people clamor for your goods. It isn't my intention to diminish her efforts. It is obvious she's very good at what she does. But business is business. If people don't like your scents, there is not a merchant around who will stock them. Nor would any customer buy them."

"It is a family business. We all contribute. I'm just a small part of it."

"You play no small part, Belle." He raked a hand through his hair, irritated with himself for treating her request as merely a pleasant distraction.

He intended to keep a close watch on her while in Oxford.

When the music stopped, he held out his arm. "Come, let me return you to your Aunt Hortensia before she comes at me with a battle mace and crushes my skull."

Belle laughed.

Her voice was sweet and lilting, and her smile reached her lovely eyes.

He put his hand over hers when she placed it on his arm. "I'll come back for you in time for the supper dance."

She nodded. "We can talk about this further."

"No, let's not. It's all conjecture right now. Let's see what unfolds in Oxford. But I've changed my mind about not having Joshua and Ronan come with me. Will you do me the favor of inviting my brothers?"

"Yes, of course." She held him back before they returned inside, looking up at him as she cleared her throat.

"What is it, Belle?"

"I have just agreed to grant your favor."

"And? Oh, hell. The protocol? *Our* protocol?" He shook his head and emitted an agonized chuckle. "No. *No.* We are not sealing it with a kiss here." She was jesting, of course. Merely teasing him about the kiss he'd given her earlier in his office. "How about I'll keep score, and we'll settle up at the end?"

She smiled. "You ought to see the look on your face. I rather enjoyed shocking you. But it's all right, Finn. I didn't really mean it."

The look she'd seen on him was not one of shock, but of inflamed desire. This is what Belle did to him. The mere possibility of kissing her set him off. What was it about her? Perhaps the book she'd mentioned Violet had given her would help explain what he was feeling. "Follow me."

He drew her down the steps into a shaded portion of the garden just beneath the veranda and took her in his arms. "Is it true, Belle?"

"Is what true?"

"Your not wanting to kiss me." It was dark where they stood, the two of them cast in shadow. But the pain in Belle's eyes stood out clearly. She thought he'd meant to put her off and never kiss her again.

Her gaze was hopeful as she studied his face. "Do you want me to *want* to kiss you?"

"Yes, I want you to indulge in as many *wants* with me as you desire. We only have another minute before I must deliver you back to your family." He kissed her lightly on the lips. "This is for granting me the favor of having my brothers join us." He kissed her again, this time pulling her up against him and crushing his lips to hers with unmasked hunger. It wasn't a gentle kiss. It wasn't a rough kiss, either. He could only describe it as profound, for this is how he felt about Belle.

Profoundly wonderful.

Profoundly hopeful.

Profoundly besotted.

He enjoyed the soft press of her mouth on his, and knew by her sigh of contentment that she was enjoying herself as well. She wrapped her arms around his neck and burrowed up against him with delightful innocence and curiosity. She tasted of the ratafia she must have sipped before dancing with him.

He felt the softness of her breasts against his chest.

When he ended the kiss, he took a deep breath to steady himself. He inhaled the scent of grass and flowers in the humid air, as well as the warm scent of lavender on Belle's skin.

"Yes, I want you to want to kiss me," he said softly. "Yes, I want to kiss you. As often as you'll permit. I didn't mean to put you off, Belle. I was only thinking of my inability to stop myself from going further if I ever did give in to your temptation."

"Going further?" Her eyes were wide in fascination. "What more are you inclined to do?"

Peel off her gown and kiss his way down her body.

He groaned. "Do you have any idea how lovely you are? You'd slap me if I told you what I'd really like to do."

He returned Belle to her family, smiled at Hortensia when she cast him that I-am-going-to-crush-your-skull look, because she was sure he was after one thing from her niece. Which he was, but if he actually succeeded in getting a night of hot, wild pleasure with exquisitely innocent Belle, he would get the special license and marry her that very same day.

Finn strode off to the card room and kept himself busy until the supper dance, first playing a few turns at whist and then settling in for the next hour playing vingt-un.

"Finn, where are you going?" Lord Crompton asked at the end of the hour when he gathered his winnings and rose to leave the table.

"Give us a chance to earn back our losses."

"Later, I've promised the supper dance to Miss Farthingale."

The Earl of Wycke, one of the foursome at their table, looked up suddenly. "Honey Farthingale?"

"No, Belle."

"They're both beautiful gels," Crompton said with a leering grin. "Well connected, but I hear they work in a shop. What's your interest in the sickly one, Brayden? Heard you saved her life at Lady Dayne's tea a few months ago. Has she been cuddling up to you since then?"

"Watch your mouth, Crompton," Wycke said, casting Finn a warning glance as well when he noticed his hands clenching. "Those girls are respectable. They'll do well for themselves. Not every man is interested in acquiring a helpless, brainless wife with impeccable bloodlines."

"Oho! You, Wycke? You'd seriously consider marrying one of them?"

"Why not, if I were in the market for a wife? Given a choice of beautiful and brainless or beautiful and clever, why wouldn't I choose clever?"

Crompton appeared surprised. "And you, Brayden? You'd choose a shopgirl over the daughter of a duke? What would your brother say? And your cousins? Why would you lower yourself to—"

"Enough about these Farthingales. Are we going to play cards or not?" Wycke raised his arm and motioned to a gentleman just entering the room. "Driscoll, come join us. We need a fourth."

Finn held back as Wycke cast him a second warning glance. He nodded to him and walked away, knowing the man was right about ignoring Crompton, much as he would have liked to pound the pompous bounder to dust.

He entered the ballroom and shouldered his way through the crowd, hoping his anger would abate by the time he reached Belle. Between Crompton's dissolute remarks about her and Walton's ogling her, he was not in good humor.

Crompton's words particularly troubled him.

Yes, he was the brother of an earl, but how did this make him anyone of note? He held no titles. He worked in finance. How was he so different from Belle? Why would working in the family perfume shops lower her standing to the point that many of the Upper Crust would shun her?

But they wouldn't dare shun him. Not only because he was very well connected. His brother Tynan was Earl of Westcliff. His cousins, Marcus and James, were the earls of Kinross and Exmoor, respectively. Their titles alone did not make them men of good character. That's just who they were, who all Braydens were raised to be. Men of honor and valor. Men who fought to protect those they loved and those too weak to protect themselves.

The Brayden women were just as valiant.

As for himself, the rich and titled valued him because of his financial prowess. His father could have been a common dustman for all they cared. Preserving their wealth, enhancing it, was all that mattered to the upper class.

He shook his head and sighed.

If any good came out of his and Belle's pretend courtship, it was that his mother would back off and stop bothering him about finding a wife.

Of course, his mother would be another one to come after him with a battle mace when she learned it was a sham.

He shook out of the thought.

Being with Belle did not feel like a sham.

Find Belle.

He'd spent the last three months doing his best to avoid her. She thought his reason was because he disliked her. It was a logical conclusion after the calamity of their first meeting. Had he ever attended a worse tea party in all his life?

But it was also the best.

One might say, frighteningly good. Well, he hadn't quite decided how he felt yet. Meeting Belle was like getting knocked down by a tidal wave and being pulled under by the force of its undercurrent.

He wasn't prepared for this feeling.

It was odd. Different.

He was used to being in control, comfortably in charge of any situation. But Belle made his senses reel out of kilter. There was something about her, an innocent sensuality is how he would describe it. She aroused him, turned him into a mindless, hungering beast.

Even amid the chaos of their first meeting, he'd felt drawn to her immediately. They had never even been properly introduced, but it hadn't stopped him from noticing her or wanting her. *Mr. Brayden, may I present to you Miss Belle Farthingale. She is here to satisfy your wildest fantasy.*

Well, only in his dreams.

Now that she'd come to him asking for help, he knew that he had to curb this inexplicable yearning for her. Spectacular fail so far. He should not have kissed her tonight. It would not do to mix business with pleasure.

It was a dangerously potent brew.

Keeping his hands off Belle while pretending to court her was not going to be easy. It wasn't a pretense for him, although he had yet to fully understand or accept these feelings roiling inside of him.

Remaining unaffected by her charm would be almost impossible, but he had to be up to the task for Belle's sake.

How was he to walk this fine line?

Perhaps if he used the time productively and learned more about her and truly got to know her. What was that old adage? Familiarity breeds contempt? He hoped so, for the sake of his peace of mind. He needed to find out all the things he did not like about her and get those nightly fantasies out of his head.

"Finn, why are you frowning?" His mother, the fierce and daunting Lady Miranda, came over to him, putting her hand on his arm to gain his attention.

"Am I?" He was impatient to reach Belle. He saw her standing beside Hortensia, fretting once more while she waited for him to claim his dance.

Did she think he'd forgotten?

"You know you're frowning. You'll scare away all the young ladies if you persist in maintaining that dark scowl." She followed his gaze. "You know Belle Farthingale, don't you? You met her at Lady Dayne's tea party."

He gritted his teeth. "Yes."

"What a mess that was. Dear me." She waved her fan, stirring the hot air. "I noticed you dancing the waltz with her earlier."

"So?"

"Is there something you wish to tell me?"

He arched an eyebrow. "Bloody hell, no."

"Finn!" She was still grasping his arm, not yet ready to let go of him. "What is your interest in the girl? I hear she has that…thing."

He tamped down his irritation. "What thing?"

No wonder the girl had a chip on her shoulder the size of an oak tree. Even his mother was passing comments about her breathing condition.

The henna-red curls on his mother's head bobbed as she shook her head. "You know very well what I mean. Weren't you the one found with your lips on hers and your hand cupping her–"

"My hand was on her heart."

"Fine, stick with that story."

He groaned. "You've been talking to Lady Withnall."

"No, she hasn't said a word to me. But others saw you. I raised you better. Why were you kissing her? Never mind. A mother doesn't really want to know."

"It wasn't a kiss. I was trying to breathe life back into her body.

Did the gossips fail to mention that?"

"They might have done. She frightened the wits out of everyone at the tea. Are you sure, Finn?"

"About asking her to dance? A wonderful suggestion." He knew he was being rude, but his own mother had no right to intrude in his private life.

He stopped before Belle. "Miss Farthingale, may I have the honor?"

She looked beautiful, soft and gentle, as she smiled up at him in obvious relief, as though worried he'd decided to abandon her.

"Yes. Thank you, Mr. Brayden."

He escorted her onto the dance floor and placed an arm around her waist. They stood side by side, he positioned slightly behind her as he took her hand in his, waiting for the cotillion to start.

What made this girl different?

She smiled up at him again.

Her cheeks were pink, and her skin felt warm. "Belle, do you want to sit this one out?"

"Afraid I'll have another breathless spell while we dance?"

Yes. "No, I just thought you might prefer to talk over our plans instead."

"You are not a smooth liar, Finn."

"Sorry, it isn't you, it's me. I feel the need for air. Truly."

She frowned and pursed her lips, now fretting. "What's wrong? It's this scheme, isn't it? You're finding it hard to pull off."

"No, Belle. Quite the opposite. I'm finding it far too easy."

Any other young lady would have accepted the compliment for what it was, but Belle's look was one of uncertainty. *Sure, you think you like me now, but just wait. I'll disappoint you.* This is what she was thinking, and it cut Finn to the bone.

"I shouldn't have kissed you tonight," he said.

She was quick to nod. "I know."

"I shouldn't have kissed you tonight because it only makes me want to steal more kisses from you." The music began before he could say more.

Since Belle was determined to prove she could make it through the dance, they stayed on the floor with the other couples. When it ended, she cast him a triumphant smile that struck him in the heart.

They moved on to supper afterward, their banter easy and constant as she nibbled her food. He steered the topic to things other than her father's ledgers, but he was worried. What would he find when they reached Oxford?

Would his sniffing around place Belle in danger?

Chapter Four

BELLE STOOD IN front of the Royal Academy, trying to rein in her excitement when she noticed Finn striding toward her. She and Honey had arrived a short while ago, driven in their uncle's carriage by the kindly coachman, Abner Mayhew. The dear man had assured them he would be back precisely at four o'clock to pick them up.

She and Honey had also been assigned a maid to escort them, a sweet but not very clever girl by the name of Elsie, who was easily distracted. Honey had dispensed with her quite handily, asking the girl if she would like to take the two hours to herself since the lecture would likely bore her to tears. "Oh, I shouldn't!"

Her sister, ever the efficient saleswoman, had cast the girl a warm, commiserating smile. "Nonsense, we're in reputable company here. I'm sure you'd enjoy a few hours to yourself."

In response, Elsie had nodded enthusiastically. "If you think it will be all right."

"We won't tell. Just make sure you're back before four o'clock when Mr. Mayhew returns with the carriage."

Simple as that, no one would realize Belle had not entered the lecture hall with her sister. "Brilliantly done," Belle whispered, the butterflies in her stomach now fluttering as Finn reached them.

"Sorry I'm late." Finn tipped a nod to Honey before turning his smile on Belle. "I was detained at my office. Hope I didn't keep you waiting too long."

Belle tried to sound casual, but she was never good at hiding her feelings and expected Finn knew she was happy to see him. "Not at all. We only arrived a few minutes ago. The lecture's just starting."

"And I had better go in and find a seat." Honey scampered inside, leaving the two of them alone on the steps.

Finn offered Belle his arm. "Shall we begin our first lesson in love?"

"Yes, let's." She tried once again to sound casual and failed miserably.

Oh, he looks so handsome. The emerald silk of his cravat accentuated the smoke-gray and dark green of his eyes, an unusual mix that held a fascinating allure. "Honey showed me where she would be sitting if we finished early, and I wanted to join her in the lecture hall. Two hours is a long time for us to chat, don't you think?"

He merely shrugged. "We'll see. It's a nice day. Care to sit in the quadrangle?"

"That would be lovely." She raised the cloth bag she was carrying. "I've brought *the* book."

He laughed and gave a mock shudder. "I am quaking in my boots. Come along, let's see what pearls of wisdom it has to offer us."

They found a bench in a quiet spot in a shaded corner of the manicured lawn.

Belle hesitated before drawing out the volume. "Finn, what if it does have magical properties? Violet said this book holds the secret to making a man fall in love."

"Are you worried we might fall in love?" He seemed to find the notion amusing but said nothing more as he waited for her to sit. He then settled beside her, stretching his long legs before him and casting her a boyishly appealing grin. Propping his shoulders on the wooden back of the bench, he closed his eyes and tipped his head toward the sun.

"I'm not worried for myself," she said, her heart aching over the impossibility of his actually having feelings for her. "You're considered

39

a catch. I, on the other hand…well, you know what everyone thinks of me."

He sighed and opened his eyes as he turned to face her. "That you're what? Smart? Beautiful? Easy to be with? Oh, the horror of it all!"

"Finn, be serious."

"I am. Go ahead and open the book to the first chapter. I'll try my best not to propose to you again. And by the way, you look beautiful. I want you to know this before we read a word. Just so you know it comes from me and not some spell you think you've cast over me out of that sorcerer's book."

"Very well." She dismissed his glib remark and turned to the first chapter. "Love does not come from the heart but from the brain. It is the brain that sends signals throughout the body, telling you what to feel. Therefore, to stimulate a man's arousal—"

Finn laughed aloud. "Hold a moment. Are you certain Violet meant to give you this book?"

Belle blushed profusely. "Perhaps this isn't such a good idea. But she said it was scientific, and the observations would all make sense once we read through it. She insisted that I read through every chapter. I tried…I started…but something always held me back."

"I'm with you now," he said gently. "We'll do this together."

She took a deep breath, hoping what Violet had told her was accurate. "Therefore, to stimulate a man's arousal response, one must arouse his sense receptacles in a pleasing way. By touch, taste, sight, smell, and hearing. Finn, I'm not sure I understand this."

He leaned closer, regarding her with patience. "It will be explained as we continue, but I think the same would apply the opposite way. For a man to win the heart of a woman, he'd have to appeal to her senses as much as she would have to appeal to his. Let's test the sense of smell. What's my scent today, Belle?"

She inhaled lightly and smiled. "Claudius again. That was easy."

She inhaled once more because she loved the scent of him. "Yes, definitely, Claudius."

"Are your sense receptacles tingling?"

If going off like fireworks was the same thing, then yes, they were. "What do you mean?"

He grinned. "Admit it, you enjoyed breathing me in. Are there butterflies fluttering in your stomach?"

Thousands.

"Not a one." Fluttering implied something mild and gentle, not a wild and mad rampage, wings crashing into stomach walls. It was not the same thing at all, so it wasn't really a lie. "Perhaps a few tingles. No fluttering."

"Then why are your cheeks suddenly red?" He put his hand over hers to stop her from slamming shut the book. "Belle, I'd probably respond the same way if I were to breathe you in. Care to have me try?"

"No." She looked up at him. "Are you making fun of me?"

He appeared genuinely surprised. "Of course not. I'm just as curious as you are. Do read on."

She eyed him warily but nodded because she was also interested in learning more. "A man's sense receptacles do not operate in quite the same way as the female's. Nor does a man's brain. It is very different from the female brain." She glanced at Finn again. "That's odd, don't you think?"

"Not so odd. Women are far more sensible than men."

"Do you think so?"

"Yes, Belle. Men often behave like idiots when they see a pretty face. They don't merely stammer or behave shyly. Their brains shut down, and other body functions seem to take over. Perhaps the book will explain it better than I can."

"Very well." She cleared her throat and continued. "When a man looks at a woman, he is making a series of quick assessments regarding her ability to bear his children. Is she too old? Too young? Too sickly or frail? And while…"

"Belle, why have you stopped?"

How could he ask? This was her, the sickly, frail creature every man would dismiss as unsuitable. She blinked, horrified her eyes were watering. She could not cry in front of Finn. But this scientific tome was stating exactly what she'd always feared.

No man would ever want her.

"Belle?"

She turned away, trying to hide her sniffles. "Isn't it obvious?"

"Not in the least."

She felt him take the book from her hands and pick up where she left off. "And while a man will ultimately peruse a woman's entire body, his first gaze is on her…" *Breasts.* He groaned. "I always wondered about that. Dare I mention that your endowments are first-rate? Because you seem to think they are somehow inferior, or that you are somehow inferior. I assure you, neither you nor they are lacking in any way."

"I'm sickly and frail. Isn't this what everyone thinks?"

"I've told you before, everyone has different strengths and weaknesses. Let me continue. And don't confuse your body parts. Lungs are not the same as your other…endowments, which as I said, are first rate."

She snorted but had to admit his ridiculous statement had effectively stopped her tears.

"Where were we? Ah, here. And while a man will ultimately peruse a woman's entire body, his first gaze is on her…"

"Why have you stopped reading?"

"The language is rather frank."

"I know, but Violet was adamant that it is important. I know you are not trying to be rude. Or lewd. Read on, and if it becomes too descriptive, we'll just read it silently together."

"Very well," he said, looking quite doubtful. But he nodded and continued. "And while a man will ultimately peruse a woman's entire body, his first gaze is on her...breasts...because they are the source of life, the source of milk for his newborn children. So, if he does not like the look of them, he will pass her over as a suitable mate."

"See, he'll pass her over."

"Belle, I see you are determined to be thick about this. How many times must I tell you? Lungs are not the same thing. An infant does not suckle his mother's lung. Shall I read on? Oh, this is rich. A man's brain functions on two levels. The low and the high. The simple and complex. When a man's brain is at its lowest function, he is only thinking of–"

"You've stopped again. Thinking of what?" She peered over his arm and gasped. *When a man's brain is at its lowest function, he is only thinking of sex.*

She felt herself blushing again.

Finn appeared to be uncomfortable as well, but he kept reading. "It is his simple brain at work, the one formed thousands of years ago at the dawn of Creation when men first walked the primeval earth. Very little thought occurs when the man's sexual urges are aroused. Perhaps no thought at all."

He glanced at her and grinned. "I can attest to that." He shook his head, gave a groaning chuckle, and pressed on. "But that is good. It is evidence of his compelling need to breed heirs with any fertile female he comes across."

"Fertile? Breeding?" She looked at him in dismay. "Finn, stop a moment. Please."

He sighed. "This book is a little too descriptive for my tastes. I can assure you, I do not intend to chase the female population of London. Nor do I regard women as broodmares. Do you want to give up on the book entirely?"

Were it any other man, her answer would be yes. But she felt safe with Finn and couldn't explain why. Nor did she wish to end their meeting, which is what would happen once they stopped reading. "Violet warned this first chapter was a bit scandalous. I had no idea how scandalous. Let's get through it as fast as possible and move on to the other chapters. She insists the observations about the five senses are very interesting, but she stressed this first chapter was important in order to understand why men and women look at things differently."

"Very well. I will say this is far more entertaining than reviewing a financial report. I had no idea men had two brains. That explains a lot about the mistakes we make, ones a woman would never make with the one brain she's been given. However, I don't know if I would consider us as having two brains, for this simple brain is little more than a hunger impulse. Perhaps more of a device that shuts off the workings of the male brain when it is starved of something it desires. But the author has obviously given thought to the feelings that compel us to do whatever it is we do."

Since the book was still open, Belle leaned over his arm and perused the next paragraph as he began to read it aloud. "Love is a higher function of the brain. The important function that makes a man feel the need to protect his family. Wife and offspring. Otherwise, he'd merely spill his seed and then move on, leaving them to be eaten by wolves."

He paused a long moment, as though considering the statement. Belle was not surprised. The need to protect was strongly ingrained in Finn. Obviously, in Romulus as well, for he hadn't hesitated to protect Violet from scandal.

"But that is why man has been given a higher brain, to enable him to love. However, before he reaches that upper function of intelligence, the man must first be attracted to the female on the simple brain level."

He paused once more and stared at her. "Well, aren't you going to ask me?"

She frowned. "Ask you what?"

He cast her another of those tenderly affectionate smiles, so that she could not remain irritated with him, even though he was having too much fun reading through the naughty bits of the chapter. "Ask me whether I'm attracted to you on a simple brain level."

She felt the heat rise in her cheeks again. Would reading this book be a constant source of embarrassment? Violet had assured the wisdom imparted was fascinating and ought to be taken to heart. "Are you attracted to me, Finn?"

"Yes, Belle."

"Why?"

He arched an eyebrow. "I couldn't tell you. That's the beauty of the simple brain. It just knows. Perhaps you and I will understand it better after we finish reading this book. Shall we read on? I think we'll have time to get through the next chapter as well. That one is about the sense of sight."

She nodded. "Violet says we often ignore what is before our very eyes. The strength of this book is it teaches us to really see what is in front of us and not formulate judgments about what we hope or expect to see. I think your financial training has given you a clarity of thought that few people can boast of."

"I don't know. Looking at numbers is quite a different thing from looking at people."

"But you seem to understand the nature of men."

He laughed. "Human nature does not change. The same sins apply to those living in the time of Ovid as those living in Shakespeare's day. Move forward about two hundred years, and here we are, sinning just as we have always done. Nothing has changed. Whether two thousand years, two hundred years, or two years ago, men still covet other men's wives and will commit adultery to satisfy their urges. People still lie, steal, even commit murder. Kings and politicians still seek to grab power. Jealousy and greed are as common today as they have ever been."

"My uncle often says people don't change, that a mean-spirited child will become a mean-spirited adult, and a good, generous child will become a good and generous adult."

"What do you see when you look at me, Belle?" He'd set the book aside and once more had his elbows propped on the back of the bench. Although his demeanor was casual, she sensed her answer was important to him.

She was afraid to tell him the truth but knew if he was to trust her now, and especially once they were in Oxford, she could only ever be honest with him. "I..." Her cheeks were in flames again. "I think you are very handsome." The most handsome man she'd ever met, but she was fairly new to London and hadn't the opportunity to meet the full crop of eligible young men yet.

However, she doubted any were better than Finn. "It isn't merely your classical good looks. It's the depth of intelligence in your eyes. It's the kindness in your smile. You are not haughty or puffed up in any way despite your obvious talent with all matters financial."

He chuckled. "There are eight Brayden boys, brothers and cousins. If one of us ever gets too full of himself, the others are there to knock sense into him. Our parents referred to us as *the wildebeests* when we were younger."

"Why is that?"

"They claimed we were wild as beasts."

She smiled. "Were you?"

"Yes, without a doubt. But to this day, as hard as we were and still are on each other, we will always band together to protect each other. Only we can beat each other up. Any outsider who tries it had better beware. He will find himself facing a wall of Braydens."

"Indeed, an impenetrable stone wall. You are all quite big. It's hard not to imagine you as Roman gladiators, fearless and ready to crush all opponents with your massive strength." When she'd lost her breath at

Lady Dayne's party and collapsed in the garden, Finn had lifted her in his arms and carried her indoors as though she weighed no more than a feather. Even in her dizzy state, she'd noticed the breadth of his chest and shoulders and the strength in his arms.

If she were to wrap both hands around his arm, she doubted her fingers would fully reach around. "How do you stay fit when your work is relatively sedentary?" she asked, truly puzzled because his lean, muscled body surely took more than moderate activity to maintain.

Then again, it was possible Finn was part man and part Greek god.

"I enjoy spending time at our country home. There's always plenty of physical work to do, clearing the fields, maintaining our barns and the homes of our tenant farmers, and repairing the grist mill. Even when at rest, we rarely stay idle. My brothers and I can usually be found riding across the countryside or swimming in our pond, or just pushing ourselves to exhaustion. If my father could have given us swords and shields and trained us as medieval knights, he would have. But my mother would have had him sleeping in the barn with the plow horses if she'd caught him."

"Goodness, we were raised so differently. The household would be in an uproar if Honey or I so much as skinned a knee or chipped a fingernail. After my first breathing attack, they decided we ought to spend more time in Oxford to be closer to doctors. Our father and uncle, my mother's brother, that is. Well, my father and uncle were trying to build up the perfume shops anyway, so we moved closer to town. Honey and I didn't mind because our mother often took us along with her to our main shop. She helped run it. She would put us in the back room to keep us out of the way, but that's where the various test fragrances were stored."

"And you began to mix and match them? Is this how they discovered your talent?"

She nodded. "I'm told my grandmother had the same ability, but she died when we were very young, so we never really knew her. The family had been trying to perfect a particular scent and couldn't figure out what was missing. I was playing around one day. I reduced some ingredients, then added a bit of essence of orange blossom. That perfume became our top seller. The adults thought it was sheer luck at first, but when I did it again, they took notice."

"Do you enjoy it, Belle?"

"Yes, for many reasons." He appeared to be listening intently and not at all bored, so she continued. "It is flattering to know that I excel at this one thing, but it also warms my heart that I can do something to help the family. There were years when my father and uncle struggled. They were too proud to ask for help from the Farthingale cousins who had made quite a name for themselves in mercantile. Uncle John's was the successful branch of the family. John and his brothers, Rupert, George, and Harrison. George went on to become a doctor, but the other brothers stayed in the business and worked to make it thrive. Rupert and Harrison often traveled to distant lands to find new fabrics, while John remained in England to run their home operation. Then Harrison went off to fight in Napoleon's war." A lump formed in her throat. "He died."

She paused a moment, recalling how badly Harrison's death had affected all of them. He had been a good man, so full of cheer and kindness. He'd left behind a young wife and baby. Of course, Farthingales took care of their own. Julia and little Harry would always be provided for and protected by the family.

Finn's hand covered hers. "It is one of the harsh realities of war. Innocent people die, good soldiers die or come home so badly wounded, they have trouble fitting in at home. This happened to my cousin, James."

"The Earl of Exmoor?"

"Yes, but his wealth and title did not protect him from the ravages of battle. Fortunately, he met and married Sophie Wilkinson, the sister of one of his friends who'd died while fighting alongside him." He removed his hand from hers and shook his head. "This discussion is getting too somber, Belle. Let's get back to the book and talk of love."

He read through the chapter on the sense of sight, then paused as he neared the end of it. "Care to know what I see when I look at you?"

"No." Belle shook her head quite vigorously. "You have to be honest with me, and I'm not certain I am thick-skinned enough to take it."

"Coward. I'm going to tell you anyway. I've already mentioned that I think you are pretty. According to this book, my *simple* brain made this assessment by a quick perusal of your body. But my brain may respond this way to many females." He ran a hand through his hair. "I don't know if that's true. You did something to me the moment I saw you."

"I did?"

"I couldn't look at anyone else after I set eyes on you. I'm still not sure why I responded to you the way I did. If this is merely a function of a simple, unthinking brain, then I should have been able to move on to ogle the other young ladies at Lady Dayne's tea."

"Didn't you?"

He cast her a wistful smile. "No. I couldn't take my eyes off you. Discretely, of course. Even when I wasn't looking, I wondered what you were doing and who you were speaking to."

"Why didn't you simply ask one of the family to introduce me to you?"

He laughed. "I was about to do just that when you disappeared from the parlor. To be honest, I wasn't certain I wanted to talk to you that afternoon. Well, I did want to. But not before I had my own feelings under control. You see, I wasn't used to approaching a young woman who intrigued me as much as you did. I hadn't yet figured out how to dazzle you with my charm and brilliance. That's when I stepped into the garden to collect my thoughts and decide what to say to you."

She winced. "Ah, yes. That was some introduction. I'm so sorry. I shall never forgive myself for the chaos I caused."

"It's the mark of a Farthingale, isn't it? Creating havoc and mayhem out of the most innocent situations." Chuckling, he took her hand again. "Do you wish to know what I thought of you afterward?"

"No, but I see you're going to tell me."

"I am." His gaze turned smoldering.

The lovely warmth already spreading through her body turned fiery.

He leaned so close, his lips were almost touching her ear. She felt his soft breath against her lobe. "What I thought was…this will make a good story to tell our grandchildren."

She leaped off the bench. "Our grandchildren?"

He rose along with her, careful to set the book aside. Goodness, what was it about him? He made her heart ache with yearning for what could never be. "Oh, Finn! Don't you see what's happening? It's that book. It is already casting its spell over you."

"Belle, I vow you are the most thick-headed young lady in existence. That book is just a book. Nothing more."

"But you said *our grandchildren.*"

He nodded. "That's right."

"Which implies we'll have children."

"I hope so."

"Which means…"

"Marriage, Belle. I hope you don't think I intended to take you on as my mistress. That will never happen."

She rolled her eyes and scurried around him to stuff the book back in its cloth wrapping. "Don't say another word. You'll regret it once you come to your senses. I'm returning this *thing* to Violet. Good riddance to it."

"You'll do nothing of the sort. Why do you think it is so impossible that a man would wish to marry you?"

Pain flashed in her eyes. "A handsome, brilliant, splendidly gorgeous, and perfect-in-every-way man like you? You are straight out of a dream. Men like you don't fall in love with girls like me."

He frowned thoughtfully. "Have you been dreaming of me, Belle?"

"That isn't the point. Our courtship is a pretense, a business arrangement to help us catch the thief who is stealing from my father. Besides, how can you want to marry me when you know so little about me? You can't possibly be in love with me yet. Love doesn't happen overnight."

"I've known you since May. It is now August. Disgustingly hot, if you ask me. And love does happen overnight. Within minutes for some. Violet and Romulus fell in love fast, in the time it took them to escape the swarm of bees. How long did that take? Minutes?"

"They are the exception to the rule."

"What rule? Love is not orderly or regimented. It strikes some of us like a bolt of lightning. Others need to take their time and think it through. Sadly, some people don't recognize it when they find it. They end up alone or marrying the wrong partner." He took her by the elbow, glancing at her hands as she clutched the cloth sack. "Our time is up. Honey's coming toward us."

"She is? Oh, I see her. Goodness, the afternoon went by so fast."

"It does when you're enjoying the company. Belle, you're right about my not intending to speak of marriage. But it has nothing to do with the book. It has to do with you and the way you see yourself. I know you're not ready to hear any of what I wish to say to you."

Honey called out to her.

She waved back, eager to end this conversation.

"Meet me here tomorrow," he said. "Same time. If it's raining, meet me inside the Royal Academy hall. I'll be there." He held her back when she sought to avoid him by walking toward her sister. "I'll always be here for you."

"No, you won't." He made her ache. He made her want to cry. He made her want things with him that she would never have. "I scare men away."

"Those men are fools."

"You're more stubborn than most. How many attacks must I suffer before you come to your senses and run away? You will run away. They all do."

"Braydens don't run."

Oh, she was going to cry.

This is pretend. It isn't going to last.

Their courtship only needed to last long enough to trick her father. "Shall we wager on it?"

CHAPTER FIVE

INN STRODE ALONG the quadrangle the following afternoon, scanning the crowd to see if Belle had arrived. His watch was attached to a fob kept in the breast pocket of his vest. He drew it out and checked the time. It was already a few minutes past two o'clock. She was late.

Had he botched matters and scared her away? He'd gone about it stupidly, making her believe he was lost under the spell of this mysterious book. That book merely explained what he was already feeling, that compelling urge to be with her for a lifetime. What he felt was genuine. His heart had responded to Belle the moment he'd met her in May.

As he pondered his next step, he saw Honey and Belle make their way through the crowd standing in front of the academy hall steps.

He emitted a breath of relief and strode toward them.

Belle had the cloth sack with her, no doubt containing the book. However, she was not smiling.

Honey nudged her forward as he greeted them. "Good afternoon, Mr. Brayden. Feel free to give my sister a swift kick in her backside if she spouts off about being unlovable. You have my hearty approval."

Belle's eyes widened in surprise. "Honey!"

Finn smiled. "I see Belle told you about yesterday's conversation."

Honey nodded. "She tells me everything."

Belle frowned. "Well, I won't make that mistake again." She

snapped her mouth shut and put her fingers to it as though to button her lips.

Finn arched an eyebrow, pleased to have an ally in Belle's sister. They both looked exceptionally pretty today. Honey's hair was a little darker than Belle's, the golden hues a little more fiery. Belle's hair was more of a tawny gold, but still contained that hint of flame. Their gowns were of a similar ivory color, but Honey had on a pale peach pelisse over hers while Belle's was moss green.

Honey was a beautiful girl, to be sure. But Belle…she turned him inside out. "Ready to start on chapter three? Which sense is that?"

"The sense of touch," Violet said from behind him, breathless as she reached them. "I sent Elsie off on a harmless errand to distract her. She'll be back soon, so we don't have much time to get you safely away. I thought I'd join Honey at the lecture while you and Belle go over the book. Am I late? Have I missed anything so far?"

Finn couldn't help but grin. "Are you speaking of the Academy program or of my time with Belle? The lecture hasn't started yet. But I see word of what Belle and I are doing is spreading around the Farthingale household like wildfire. I suppose you were there when Belle confided in her sister."

She nodded. "I was. We tell each other everything."

Oh, lord! He'd better remain on his best behavior around Belle. It wasn't going to be easy. She brought out the hot and wicked, simple brain mating urges in him. "Honey just mentioned the same to me. This cannot go further than the three of you. No one else can know."

Violet's eyes widened as she regarded him in earnest. "I wouldn't dream of repeating your plan to anyone else, nor would I ever interfere. Do take Belle away, and go on about your business. Honey and I will see you after the lecture. Oh, and be careful with the sense of touch. It seems harmless, but it isn't really." She whispered something to Honey as the two of them scurried up the steps into the Royal Academy hall, their heads bowed, and the two of them giggling.

Belle began to nibble her lip furiously.

He took her arm to escort her to a quiet corner. "You'll make your lip bleed if you don't stop fretting."

"How can I stop? You heard what Violet said. Touch is dangerous."

"It doesn't have to be. I'll touch you gently."

She shook her head and groaned. "Oh, Finn. That's the most dangerous of all. You mustn't be gentle with me. I mean, you ought to be gentle, but you mustn't...perhaps it is safest not to test it out at all."

"Then how are we to experience the sensations the author of this book wishes to convey to us?"

They found the same empty bench under the shade tree. Finn remained standing while Belle took a seat. She looked up at him, her gaze almost pleading. "Let's set it aside for now."

"Let's not. We have already touched, although not with the awareness one has when concentrating only on the person beside them. Surely you know I'd never hurt you."

She nodded. "I know you wouldn't purposely."

"Here's a compromise. Let's read through the chapter, and then we can decide if we wish to experiment with this sense." He sank onto the bench beside her. "All right? Let's see where this takes us."

He tried not to respond to her nearness as she leaned close to read silently along with him. But it proved difficult. All of his senses were going off like fireworks. Belle's scent of sweet lavender reminded him of a gentle breeze in a Highland meadow. Her body was sheer temptation, and he almost leaped out of his skin when her shoulder accidentally grazed his arm.

When she realized she'd drawn too close, she hastily drew back with a muttered apology.

"Don't apologize for what comes naturally between the two of us." But it was more than that to Finn. She stirred something deep within him, something innate and primal that not even he fully understood.

They had yet to discuss the sense of hearing, but ripples of pleasure tore through him every time she gasped or laughed or spoke up about one thing or another. The sense of sight was perhaps the most devastating of all, for she grew more beautiful each time he saw her. He wasn't certain why. She hadn't changed her appearance. She wore her hair the same way, dressed the same way, hadn't grown any taller, nor had the shape of her body changed.

So, what made her more beautiful?

Perhaps this next chapter would explain it to him.

"Finn, how silly of me," she said after they had read to the end of the chapter. "No wonder Violet warned us about this sense. I only considered the touch of our hands, but there are other ways we can touch each other. I hadn't thought of the touch of our lips."

He laughed. "It's the first thing that came to my mind." He'd kissed her lightly when sealing their agreement on the sham courtship and again the other night in the garden, perhaps not so lightly that time. Still, he had done his best to hold himself back.

Their courtship would be no sham if he had any say in the matter. The mere brush of his lips to hers had sent his body into a hot spiral. What would happen when he truly gave free rein to his desires and kissed her as he'd fantasized?

Perhaps this was his low brain function taking over again, because he could not get the thought out of his mind. If he wasn't careful, the ache to kiss her would become an obsession. Who could blame him?

He turned to Belle.

Her lips were puckered in thought.

They were perfect lips. Beautifully shaped. Soft to the touch. "I'm going to kiss you properly this time, Belle."

He wouldn't blame her if she struck him over the head with the book.

She looked up at him, her eyes wide in alarm. "Here? Now? And what would you call last night's kiss?"

Dark clouds were gathering overhead, now threatening rain. Had he not been so caught up in reading the chapter on the sense of touch, he might have noticed everyone clearing out of the quadrangle and hurrying indoors.

He shut the book and stuck it in the sack, then took Belle's hand. "Let's go inside before we are drenched."

They made it into the Royal Academy just as the first drops of rain began to fall. "Oh, dear. I didn't bring my umbrella," she said, gazing out one of the tall windows as rain began to pelt against it. "Honey didn't think to bring hers either. And I didn't see Violet carrying one."

"These afternoon downpours never last long. The sun will be shining again by the time the lecture is over, and they find us."

She nodded. "What shall we do in the meanwhile? We could catch the last part of the lecture."

"No." He still held her hand. Her gloved hand, for she hadn't taken off her ivory lace gloves as they'd been reading. They were light and appropriate for a summer outing. He still hated the barrier they created between his palm and her soft skin. "There are plenty of rooms throughout the building. Old naval offices. Art studios. Probably a small library."

"Where we can continue reading?" As they'd run inside the building, the quickening wind had swept a curl or two of her hair out of place.

Finn couldn't resist touching her to nudge the wisps back in place. As he finished, his knuckles grazed her cheek in a gentle caress. "We'll do that as well."

She licked her lips. "As well? What else are we going to do?"

"I told you. I'm going to kiss you deeply and unrestrainedly."

"Must you?"

He sighed. "No, Belle. Not if you don't want me to."

"Honesty in all things," she muttered, her cheeks turning fiery as she met his gaze. "I want you to. Of course, I do."

His tension eased, and he cast her a tender smile. "So do I, but you already know that. There's a small naval library just down the hall. It hasn't been in use since the Royal Navy's administrative offices were brought into the Admiralty. If we're alone, I'll kiss you behind the stacks. No one will see us. If we're not alone, then we can simply chat and enjoy each other's company."

The door was unlocked when Finn tried it. But he did not take Belle inside until the hallway had cleared, so there was no one to see them. For his part, he didn't care if they were caught alone. He knew he wanted Belle.

But Belle had not yet made her decision.

He knew she liked him, perhaps felt something more for him. But she could not get out of her own way to release those doubts about herself and see herself for the wonderful person she was. Right now, she was more comfortable believing this courtship was a pretense and would be over once he figured out who was stealing from her father.

If it eased her mind to think so, he was not going to make an issue of it now.

But this was no pretense to him.

He had yet to figure out why but supposed the answers would come to him as they continued reading that book. It wasn't magical, but it did have insights into the workings of the mind that he found quite intriguing.

The library was musty, and the books obviously had not been touched in months. Dust had collected on the stacks. Finn worried Belle might breathe it all in. Little motes floated in the air. They were a mere nuisance to him, perhaps might evoke a sneeze out of him. But what damage would they cause to Belle's lungs?

She must have read his thoughts. "I'll be all right, Finn."

He frowned. "Are you certain?"

She nodded. "Yes. I'm with you. I know you'll take care of me if something happens. But it won't happen."

His frown deepened. "How can you be sure?"

"Because I feel safe with you. If I start to cough, we'll just leave. Fear or panic is what sets off my attacks. I'm not afraid of anything when I'm with you." She regarded him for a long moment, appearing startled by the realization. Finally, she smiled at him. "I like having my very own gladiator to protect me."

He wanted to tell her he would always be there to protect her, but she was not ready to think of him as a part of her life beyond these next few weeks.

"We won't be in here very long," he assured, mostly to warn himself not to share more than a steamy kiss or two. She wasn't ready for more.

But he was.

He wanted to devour her. He supposed this was his low brain function taking control again.

He led her behind the third row of shelves and took the reticule holding *The Book of Love* from her hands. He set it on one of the empty shelves and drew her up against him. He noticed that her eyes were wide with trepidation as he circled his arms around her.

He held her lightly, so as not to hold her captive. He wanted Belle to understand she could pull away at any time.

However, it pleased him that she did not seem inclined.

She slid her hands up his chest to circle them around his neck. "I'm ready."

"Close your eyes."

He watched them flutter closed and took another moment to study her face even down to the freckles on her nose. "You're beautiful, Belle," he said, and was about to lower his mouth to hers when the door suddenly opened and what sounded like two people frantically whispering to each other hurried in.

Belle opened her eyes and stared up at him in alarm.

Lord! They couldn't be caught in here together. But there was no way to escape without being seen. They had no choice but to wait until these two intruders left. How long would it take?

He gazed at Belle, hoping she would not panic.

Apparently, maintaining eye contact with her seemed to reassure her.

But whatever relief either of them might have felt soon turned to embarrassment as they realized what this couple had rushed in here to do. Believing the naval library abandoned, they had stolen in for an assignation.

From what Finn could gather from their whispers, the woman was married, but not to the gentleman who accompanied her.

Hen's teeth.

They began to have sex on one of the tables. The sort of hungry, animal, groping…never mind. Their grunts and groans could not be ignored or mistaken for anything other than a noisy climax.

Belle's face was in flames.

Finn kept her in his arms and had her just look at him. The pair finished rather quickly, to his way of thinking. If he ever had Belle in that situation, he wouldn't merely be shoving himself into her and finishing fast.

He shook out of the thought. He would never be with Belle in such circumstances. Married to others? Clandestine meetings for quick sex? Desperate and unhappy? The strangers righted themselves and stole out, leaving him and Belle alone once more.

Belle looked as though she wanted to cry.

Finn groaned. "We are nothing like that couple. You are not a sordid assignation for me. I hope you know this."

She managed an unconvincing nod.

"I'm so sorry, Belle. This is all my fault. I should not have brought you in here. Blame it on my low brain. I wanted to kiss you. I wanted to hold you in my arms. But this feels wrong. I'm not going to kiss you in some musty back room. You deserve better."

"Let's go, Finn." She eased out of his arms and took a step back.

He nodded, still kicking himself for his stupidity. The unhappy couple and their desperate, clandestine groping were a warning to him. "When I kiss you again, it will be in a rose-scented garden under a silver moon."

"You've already done that. Please, let's go."

He stepped around her and walked to the door, carefully opening it to peer into the hall. "Belle, I'm not ashamed of my feelings for you. The kisses we've shared were heartfelt and real. But they were also restrained. I purposely held back because you are innocent, and I wanted to make you feel comfortable around me."

"I appreciate your explanation, but I don't think we ought to kiss again. We aren't meant to be. Isn't it obvious? The couple who interrupted us moments ago, they were an omen, a warning that we shouldn't be doing this."

"That we shouldn't be falling in love? Why? Because you think you are unlovable?"

"I don't wish to talk about it."

She was overset, not that he blamed her. He knew better than to press her about her feelings now. "I'll take you back to Honey."

Once he was certain the hall was empty, he escorted her to the lecture hall where her sister and Violet were listening to a renowned scholar on ancient Greece. He was about to open the door when Belle suddenly gasped. "The book! We left it on the shelf! Oh, Finn. I can't lose it. Violet will never forgive me. We have to go back."

He placed a hand lightly on her elbow to calm her. "I'll get it. Wait here. The audience is applauding, so I think the lecture is about to end. Find Honey and Violet. Stay with them until I return."

She looked so unhappy, he couldn't bear it. This was his fault. He'd taken the reticule from her hands and stuck it on a shelf. What had he been thinking to take her into that old library? And for what?

To steal a kiss she wasn't ready to accept?

He found the reticule where he'd left it. "Thank goodness," he muttered, checking to make certain the book was still in there. To his relief, it was.

He tucked it under his arm and strode out, only to bump into the Earl of Wycke. The earl was just as surprised to see him but cast him a wry grin. "Brayden, I hadn't expected to see you outside your office at this hour." He glanced at the reticule tucked under his arm. "I gather that isn't yours."

"No, just retrieving it for a friend."

Wycke arched an eyebrow. "Does this friend of yours happen to be a Farthingale?"

He ignored the question. "Good to see you, Wycke. Thank you for handling Lord Crompton the other night."

"The oaf was out of line. Ah, but I see you have been spending time with the Farthingales. They're coming this way."

Finn followed Wycke's gaze to the one dark head and the two golden heads bobbing through the crowd toward them.

Apparently, Violet knew Lord Wycke. She greeted him warmly and explained their acquaintance to the rest of them. He and his family had been guests at Sherbourne Manor. Violet's sister, Poppy, was married to Nathaniel Sherbourne, the Earl of Welles.

She introduced her cousins to Wycke and then asked after his family. "Ann is deliriously happy," he replied. "She and Malcolm will be coming to town in October. I'm looking forward to it. My mother now has a companion to assist her, but it isn't the same. She misses Ann terribly."

Violet nodded solemnly. "I have been remiss. Would you mind if I paid a call on her? Is tomorrow too soon?"

Wycke chuckled. "Not soon enough. Visit any time you wish. As often as you wish. Your cousins are welcome to accompany you. She could do with some merriment. Seeing your cheerful faces would be just the thing."

They agreed to visit Lady Wycke at noon tomorrow.

Finn said nothing, merely watched as Wycke strode out of the building. The rain had tapered to a drizzle, more of a sun shower now, for the clouds were breaking up, and large patches of blue were visible in the sky. "I suppose this rules out our meeting tomorrow," he said to Belle.

Violet was the one to respond. "Not at all. We'll stay no more than an hour with Lady Wycke. Belle will meet you here as usual."

Belle did not appear happy about it but did not contradict her cousin.

That's all Finn cared about, to see her again, to touch her again and allow her laughter to warm his soul. Gad, he was mindless over this girl. "Tomorrow it is."

He was about to hand the book to Belle, but she shook her head. "Keep it. Bring it with you when I see you next."

He eyed her curiously. "Belle, there's no magic within its pages. It hasn't cast a spell over either of us. Foisting it off on me won't change anything."

Even if there was a spell to break, how would putting the book in *his* hands help? He wasn't going to suddenly fall in love with some duke's vapid daughter. But he liked the idea of reading it on his own, for reading with Belle was not working out at all. He would finish the book this evening in the quiet of his bedchamber.

He hoped it would answer the question burning in his mind: How do I make Belle fall in love with herself?

CHAPTER SIX

FINN STOPPED AT White's for a drink with his brother before heading home. He was eager to read the book, but he also wanted Tynan's opinion on this matter of love. Tynan was happily married, but his courtship of Abigail had not been easy due to her difficult family circumstances.

He hoped to gain some insight into breaking through the wall of doubt Belle had built around herself. "Tynan, thank you for meeting me here."

"I'm always available for you, little brother." He gave Finn a hearty clap on the back and laughed, for Finn was the tallest of the Braydens, and Tynan's referring to him as his *little brother* was purposely provoking and irksome, but in a loving way.

"You know I can kick your sorry arse, Ty."

"But you won't because you adore and admire me." He then motioned toward a quiet corner of the club's main room. "Let's sit over there. No one will disturb us."

The wood-paneled chamber was filled with comfortably padded wing chairs and small tables between them where one could set down a drink or newspaper. The carpeting was thick and absorbed most of the sound in the room.

Tynan ordered the steward to bring a brandy for each of them and waited for the man to leave before leaning forward to begin their private conversation. "You don't look happy, Finn. What's wrong?"

Finn stared into his brandy, saying nothing for a long while. Since he was not particularly thirsty, he merely swirled the glass in his hand, watching the dark amber liquid catch the firelight and shimmer within the finely cut crystal. "I'm not good at this courtship business."

Tynan arched an eyebrow. "What makes you think I was any more adept at it than you?"

"Abigail married you, so you must have done something right."

Tynan shook his head and chuckled, but after a moment, he turned serious. "It was purely accidental. I had no clue what I was doing. It took me a while to even realize I was courting her. At first, she was merely a distraction from my boredom. Well, that doesn't sound quite right. I was looking for something more in life. To be of use to someone other than myself. When I saw her, I knew she was my purpose. I wanted to protect her from her family troubles."

Tynan paused to take a sip of his drink before continuing. "Abby's family life was dismal. Even so, she refused my help. I liked that strength in her. But it only made me more determined to see her through her troubles. I stopped by every day, at first because I wanted to keep a protective eye on her. Then I stopped by every day because I felt a part of me was missing when I did not see her."

Finn sat back and listened.

It took him a moment to digest what his brother had said about Abby being a missing part of him. Yes, this is how he was coming to feel about Belle. It had started from the moment he'd touched his lips to hers to breathe life back into her body. He'd been trying to save her life back then, but with each breath he forced into her lungs and each press of his hand to her chest, it was as though he was claiming a piece of her heart and tucking it away in his.

He'd purposely avoided her for three months because he felt so out of control whenever he saw her. Yet, he'd quietly looked for her at every ball, every musicale, and every *ton* party. He'd needed that glimpse of her and felt out of joint when she failed to attend a particular affair.

He dared not mention this to Tynan. He trusted his brother, of course. But men did not discuss their *feelings*. He wasn't looking for commiseration. He was trying to understand logically why the mere sight of Belle turned him upside down. He was interested in the mechanics of love, curious how to recognize it, build on it. He knew it was not the same as building a catapult or breaking it down by every beam and bolt.

He was also trying to understand why he'd avoided the pleasures of other women ever since meeting Belle. The entire first chapter in *The Book of Love* explained why males were guided by their low brain instincts to mate with as many fertile females as possible. Yet, he'd known within moments that he wanted no one but Belle.

Why?

Perhaps the explanation was as Tynan had just said. Belle was that missing part of him. How was he to convince her of it? "She is pushing me away. She's afraid to fall in love with me."

His brother frowned. "Then it's serious between the two of you."

Finn grunted. "For my part, yes…I think so."

Tynan's frown deepened. "You have to be sure, Finn. She isn't a toy you can toss in a box and forget about once you're through playing. You have to know you love her, have to feel it deep in your soul. Abby was fragile when I met her. I could have broken her so easily. It seems Belle is the same way. I knew Abby was right for me. My lack of doubt helped ease her doubts."

Finn absorbed what his brother was saying.

Tynan set down his drink and leaned forward again. "It may be that Belle is sensing your uncertainty, not hers."

"Perhaps." Finn ran a hand through his hair in consternation. Had he been casting blame on Belle when the fault was with him? He knew she was someone special, but was he truly ready for that lifetime commitment?

"Ah, but you're the logical brother." Tynan was now smirking at him. "You need to think everything through, study the viability of a venture from every angle."

"What's wrong with that? I've been successful at it."

"Love is not a business transaction. Marriages can be made for business reasons and commonly are, but love is factored out of the equation in such cases. If you feel the need to set down reasons for and reasons against loving Belle, then you're not ready. Love is complicated. Think of it as stars aligning in the sky. You both need to be ready to accept each other, to pledge your fealty to each other."

"I think Belle wants it, but she fears it. Even if she trusted me, she'd still doubt."

Tynan sighed. "I've been through it. Abby was afraid she'd disappoint me. She was certain I would come to my senses and want out of the marriage. I had to convince her it wouldn't ever happen."

"How?"

"I don't know, but as you mentioned, it starts with trust. Once you trust in your feelings, she'll start to trust in them, too. There's more to a successful marriage. But you're my little brother and have delicate ears."

"Blessed saints, Ty. Enough already." But he shook his head and laughed because he wasn't really irritated. "I've been bigger than you since I turned sixteen. Tell me everything you know about the elements of love. I need information."

"Love isn't merely about physical attraction, although Abby and I..." He cleared his throat and grinned smugly.

Finn groaned. "Shut up. I don't need that much detail. Certainly not about your antics in the marital bedchamber."

"Marriage has to be built on mutual respect, shared goals, and friendship. But there also must be intimacy, so the physical contact cannot be overlooked. It enhances everything."

Finn nodded. Didn't he desire intimacy with Belle? He wanted to wrap her in his arms, wanted to share his bed with her, and explore her delectable body. He also wanted to confide in her, share a life with her. He set down his brandy and rose. "Thank you, Ty. This has been helpful."

His brother rose along with him. "You know you can always turn to me."

Finn nodded. "I know."

He returned home and went straight to his bedchamber. His mother was hosting a small dinner party. He had no intention of joining her and her friends for an insipid evening of polite conversation, although his mother was not quite the model of discretion. She could be fiery when indignant. *Hell hath no fury like Lady Miranda on a crusade.* Joshua and Ronan would attend. Their presence would ensure he would not be missed.

Finn undressed and fell into bed with Belle's book in hand. Before he knew it, he was absorbed in reading. In truth, each chapter opened his eyes to what he had been missing...or rather, what he had been overlooking because of preconceived notions of what things ought to be. The chapters on the senses were interesting, but it was the discussion on how one built bonds of commitment that he found fascinating. Shared values. Shared goals. Compatible behaviors.

This is what Ty had been talking about, and it struck him as quite fascinating.

He hadn't given thought to "taking a wife" beyond knowing that someday he would marry. But who? And why? What was it about Belle that appealed to him beyond her looks, which were enhanced or dismissed depending on his senses? Sight, touch, and so on.

Even if everything about Belle pleased his senses, there was more to consider. The *ton* was rife with gossip about Lord M's excessive drinking. Lord P's excessive gambling. Lady B's string of lovers. But what of unhappy couples whose behavior was not excessive, but merely incompatible? There were just as many of those. A lord who preferred country life to that of town, while his wife found herself bored to tears in the country and yearned for escape to London. Or the other way around. Or a frugal man with a wife who loved to spend. Or a man whose spending needed to be reined in?

There were so many little things that could undermine the initial attraction. A man with no sense of humor, who never laughed, married to a woman who appreciated a good laugh. Or a prankster who irritatingly never stopped joking around.

The more Finn read on, the more he realized just how fragile happiness could be and how easily one could face disillusionment. Yet, despite all, there were many happy marriages. As far as he could tell, they were still in the majority, even among arranged marriages. Perhaps it had to do with expectations. When entering an arranged marriage, one did not expect to fall wildly in love with one's spouse. One merely hoped to get along, to not find the spouse too repulsive to tolerate. They went from fearing the worst to appreciating their good fortune in finding a mate they could rely on to build a life and family.

Developing that intimacy was important. But sex and love were not the same thing. He knew where to go when in need of sex. He hadn't been to those places since meeting Belle. He didn't fully understand why he'd suddenly turned into a monk.

He still had urges, but they were subtly different now.

Meeting Belle had changed him.

He wanted sex *and* intimacy.

More important, he wanted them only from her.

It was well into the wee hours of the morning by the time he finished reading the book. His mind was racing, so he had trouble falling asleep. The next thing he knew, Ronan was pounding on his door. "Finn, aren't you up yet? Come on. The carriage is ready. Move your arse, or you're going to make me late."

Bollocks.

"Give me twenty minutes," he said with a groan, barely able to raise his head. Indeed, it was all he could do to crawl out of bed.

This was unlike him. He usually rose early, got himself ready, managing to shave, wash, and dress without the assistance of a valet, which is why he, Ronan, and Joshua shared one valet among the three of them. Fortunately, Harrigan entered right behind Ronan, ready to help him prepare for the day.

Harrigan had been a sergeant in his cousin James's regiment, which explained why he was now barking orders at Finn. The man was gruff and no-nonsense, not at all what one would expect of a valet, but his mother had taken to him at once, and there was no contradicting Lady Miranda once she had her mind made up. "My boys are little better than animals," she'd told Harrigan when engaging his services. "Do what you must to keep them in line."

Despite his gruff exterior, Harrigan had a soft heart. Most of the time, he was more of a mother hen than a drill sergeant. But he was efficient. Finn, who had yet to fully open his eyes, found himself properly groomed and attired, ready to meet the day within said twenty minutes.

He started to march downstairs when he remembered the book.

He did not wish to tote it around with him all day, so he handed it to a footman with instructions to deliver it to Belle. "Number 3 Chipping Way. Make certain it is given directly into Miss Belle Farthingale's hands."

"I'll take care of it at once," the man assured.

Finn nodded his thanks and strode outside to climb into the waiting carriage. As he hopped in, he noticed Ronan's belongings being packed atop it. "Are you going somewhere?"

His brother grunted. "Where's your mind been lately? I'm headed to Penrith. One of mother's friends is having some difficulty managing her farm. It's a pretty patch of land in the Lake District, so I'm told. Mother is convinced someone is purposely trying to ruin her friend and chase her off the land."

"Oh, right. She's been going on about it all week. Why send you now? I wanted you to come with me to Oxford."

"Belle's house party? Sorry, Finn. I can't. Besides, those beautiful Farthingales are more dangerous than any rogues I may encounter. I'd like to remain a bachelor for several more years. Not in any hurry to shackle myself." Ronan shook his head. "Joshua will accompany you. Not that I'm adverse to meeting beautiful young ladies, but you know how it is. Mother grabbed me at supper last night. Joshua, the coward, kept his head bowed low and refused to meet her gaze."

Finn laughed. "You should have done the same."

"She was going to choose one of us for the task, no matter what we said or did. An irate Miranda is a tempest that cannot be avoided or ignored. So, it was Joshua or me, since you were hiding in your bedchamber. She's been insufferable lately, going on about her poor friend. I knew it was going to be me she chose."

"Why?"

"Because I opened my big mouth. I told her to go up there herself if she was that incensed."

Finn laughed. "Do you have a death wish?"

"I guess I do. After she clubbed me over the head with her fan, she realized it wasn't such a bad idea to send reinforcements to her friend. I'm heading up there as soon as I drop you off at your office. You'll have to make your own way home."

"I'm a big boy. I'll manage." Finn shook his head and laughed again. "Good luck, Ronan." But he tempered his laughter with some sober words of caution. "Will you take a Bow Street runner or two up with you? If Mother's right and there is someone trying to swindle her friend, then you might be in danger."

He nodded. "I'll nose about quietly on this trip. If there's trouble, I'll send word. What about you? Why a house party in Oxford? I never knew you to accept those invitations before. Is it Belle Farthingale? How serious are you about her?"

Finn ignored the question.

The expression on his face must have given him away, for Ronan's eyes widened in surprise. "Let me know if I should return for a wedding."

"There's little chance of it. Belle still needs convincing."

"Lay on the Brayden charm. She'll be falling into your arms before you know it."

Finn wished his brother well, reminded him to send word immediately if he sensed danger, then stepped down from the carriage once it drew up in front of his office. He had trouble concentrating on his work, his attention constantly diverted by the ticking clock on his mantel. He was impatient for two o'clock to approach.

Finally, at quarter to the hour, he set down his quill pen, told his clerks he'd return in a few hours, and walked off to meet Belle. Even if they made no further progress on *The Book of Love*, she still had to be seen with him if her father was to believe their courtship ruse when they reached Oxford.

He saw two golden-haired heads bobbing in the distance and breathed a sigh of relief. Belle had come. He wasn't certain she would. "Good afternoon," he said, escorting her and Honey into the Royal Academy building.

He noticed Belle did not have the book with her.

"I decided not to bring it. But thank you for returning it to me. Did you manage to read it in its entirety?"

He nodded.

"Was it helpful?"

"It was interesting. Yes, perhaps helpful. That remains to be seen. We don't need it today."

She arched an eyebrow in surprise. "We don't?"

"No." He stood beside her as her sister and maid walked in to take their seats in the lecture hall. "We don't even have to talk. We can stay for the lecture if you wish."

"But that would be a waste of two hours when we could be learning about love."

"And learning more about each other." He nodded in agreement. "But you have to be open to it, Belle. I'm not happy about what happened yesterday. I wanted to kiss you, but I went about it all wrong."

She sighed. "I could have objected at any point but didn't. I wanted to kiss you, too."

He smiled at her. "Well, that's progress."

"I'm sorry I left the book at home."

He placed her arm in his and escorted her outdoors to their usual bench. "The chapters on the five senses are not difficult once you understand that looking at someone, or hearing what that person is saying, and so on, needs to be done without a cloud of judgment."

"Much like distilling a fragrance to its essence."

"Yes, very much so. Strip away everything but its purest kernel." He sank onto the bench beside her. "I'm an organized person. I've been known to make lists for business decisions. The pros and cons of an acquisition or a sale. I've never made lists on matters of love. But I think it will be helpful for us. Shall I start?"

"Very well, but will this be a general list or one specific to me?"

"Specific to you, Belle. You're the reason I'm here. You're the reason I stayed up all night reading that book. You're the reason I look forward to our afternoon meetings. I'd find a thousand excuses not to be here if it were anyone else."

Her eyes widened, for he'd surprised her again. "I'm flattered."

Why was she always surprised when he complimented her? This disappointed him. She had to know he cared for her. "You don't really believe me. What's holding you back? Do I appear untrustworthy?"

"Not at all, Finn." A rosy blush spread across her cheeks. "You know why I can't…"

"Ah, those delicate lungs of yours. You still believe I can make a list running on two pages of all your positive attributes, but this one negative completely erases them all. What if I told you I have a bad heart? That I could very well be dead by the age of thirty."

"Oh, Finn! Is it true?" She placed a hand on his arm in a natural gesture of comfort.

"Would it make a difference in how you felt about me?"

"Only in how quickly I'd move matters along. Knowing there's limited time, every moment has to be precious."

"But if you loved me, you wouldn't turn me down because of it if I proposed to you?"

"No, I—"

"Then why won't you believe I feel the same about you?"

"It's different." She gave a stubborn shake of her head.

"Not different. It's exactly the same thing. Despite what the damn book says, I'm not looking to marry a body part. But I'm not here to argue with you, Belle. Tell me more about yourself."

"What do you wish to know?"

He shrugged. "Whatever you wish to tell me. What were you like as a little girl? What are your hopes and dreams? What do you enjoy doing? What irritates you? What intrigues you? You can even tell me how today's visit was with Lady Wycke. Pick any topic."

"And you'll *listen*?"

He cast her a soft smile. "With my ears and my heart."

CHAPTER SEVEN

B ELLE HATED WHEN Finn said nice things to her. Well, she didn't really, but it only pointed out how perfect he was, and how could he possibly like her as much as he did?

Violet had mentioned the Brayden men were honorable, not the sort to fawn over women or spout poetry because this was expected in the game of conquest.

No, these Braydens were straightforward and no-nonsense, in a heartwarming, sweep-you-off-your-feet way.

She saw this in Finn, and it frightened her.

He sighed, regaining her attention. "Start talking, Miss Farthingale. The lecture will be over before we've accomplished anything."

She even liked the gentle, teasing way he nudged her. This was one of the many things she adored about him. He had an intimidating frown and a severe manner about him, but he was never that way with her, only playful and coaxing. "I don't know what to say about myself."

He grinned. "Yes, you do. You just don't like to talk about yourself. May I add, this is an admirable trait. Most people are more than happy to chatter on and on about themselves, boring others to tears. It is often the ones you want to hear from who keep silent, such as you. Please, Belle. Tell me whatever you wish about yourself. It can be something frivolous, but I hope you'll tell me something important. Something you feel is significant to you."

"Will you do the same?"

He nodded. "Yes, I promise."

She nibbled her lip, finding it hard to talk about herself. But it was important for Finn to learn all about her. Then he'd understand why he had to forget her and move on. "Very well. I shall start at the very beginning. I was born before my time. I mean, physically speaking. I wasn't due to be born for at least another month. I arrived early. My parents were not sure I would survive."

Finn cast her a smile that shot straight to her heart. "But you did. You were a little fighter."

She rolled her eyes. Why did he always do this? Turn a fault into a compliment? "I was a sickly child. My family wasn't certain I would survive beyond my childhood."

"And yet, here you are."

She frowned at him. "They had to change their lives because of me, moving closer to Oxford because I seemed to be sensitive to everything in the countryside. Hay, grass, flowers, cattle."

"And had they not done this, they might never have discovered your talent for fragrances, and might not now be running the most successful—"

"Gad! Why are you so chirpy? You look like a Viking warrior, someone more comfortable carrying a battle axe to crack heads open if anyone dares speak to you before you've had your breakfast. Yet, here you are, twisting everything I say into something rosy and cheerful. Do you spring out of bed, humming a sprightly tune every morning? Or fall asleep every night with the drapes open, so the sunshine hits your face as it rises to mark the start of a new day?"

He stretched his arm across the back of the bench and eased closer. "No one has ever called me chirpy before. I am not *chirpy*. I sleep with the drapes closed. I bite off people's heads if they chatter at me before I've read my morning newspaper. Have you ever considered that you're the one twisting my words? If I said you are beautiful, how would you respond?"

She swallowed hard. Her instinct was to say *no, I'm not.* Even though he was regarding her sternly, she could see the tenderness in his gaze. She tried not to smile but couldn't help it. "I'd say, of course I am beautiful. I'm so amazingly beautiful, I outshine the sun. Indeed, the sun weeps before me, for it pales in comparison to my dazzling magnificence. I'm so beautiful, tulips pour from my lips whenever I speak, and roses spout from my arse whenever I—"

"Belle!" He burst out laughing. "Well done. Go on, tell me more."

"Isn't this enough?" She felt the heat rising in her cheeks, for she'd never spoken so boldly to a man in her entire existence.

He shook his head. "Not nearly enough. Tell me about your eyes."

"My vision is good. I don't wear spectacles."

He leaned back and groaned. "Were you always this contrary as a child? No, say something poetically nice about your eyes."

"Isn't that your job? To flatter innocent debutantes and make them swoon at your feet. You want me to spout drivel? Besides, I don't look at my eyes. I don't know what other people see in them."

He drew close once again, his gaze hot enough to melt the bench where they were seated. "Very well then, let me describe your eyes. They sparkle like blue diamonds. But they aren't cold like those gems. They're warm and inviting. I see kindness and compassion in them. I see intelligence and impudence. Most of all, I see a vulnerable beauty."

She sighed. "Let's move on to your hopes and dreams. What do you wish for in life, Finn?"

He arched an eyebrow. "We're still on you. How about you answer the question you posed. What do you want most in life?"

She clasped her hands together as they rested on her lap and stared down at them. "To be happy. Isn't this what most people wish for."

He teased a curl at her ear. "Yes, I would think so. And what will make you happy? Truth, Belle. This is what your *Book of Love* is all about, sharing yourself with the person you wish to make your partner for life. I read it cover to cover last night. This is important to us."

"Us?" She cleared her throat.

"Yes, *us*. You can pretend this isn't real. But don't expect me to play along."

"You aren't one for playing games, are you?"

His lips curled upward in the hint of a smile. "No."

"Um, will you repeat the question?"

He chuckled. "You're stalling, but very well. This isn't a test…well, perhaps it is in a way. But there is no right or wrong answer. Nor does it have to be a deep or meaningful answer. It can be something in the moment, a whim or fancy. Don't think too hard about it. Answer with your heart, that's all you need to do. What will make you happy, Belle?"

She was still staring down at her lap. "Kissing you, I should think."

His breath caught, for he hadn't expected this answer. Yet, it pleased him beyond anything else she could have said. "That's an amazing coincidence. I was thinking the same thing about you."

She looked up, startled. Ever so slowly, her expression began to relax until she was smiling at him. He wanted to take her in his arms then and there and plant a scorching kiss on her beautiful lips. But he noticed Honey approaching. "Timing is everything," he muttered and eased away.

"Oh, Finn. What were we thinking? We couldn't have done anything about it here anyway." Belle was as disappointed as he was, but she pasted a too-bright smile on her face as her sister approached.

"We'll take this up tonight at Lord Goring's musicale," he said, glancing beyond her shoulder. "Your sister is overset. I wonder what's happened."

Belle jumped to her feet and rushed toward Honey. "What's wrong?"

"Father's been hurt. Only a sprained ankle and some bruises. Uncle Rupert happened to be in Oxford and heard about it. He couldn't stay long with Father because he had meetings in Carlisle and had to leave that very day, but he wrote to Uncle John to convey his alarm. Now, Uncle John has sent Abner Mayhew with the carriage to bring us home right away. He must suspect there is something more than an accidental trip and fall going on." She glanced at Finn. "I don't know what to do. Shall we cancel our house party?"

"No. It seems more important than ever to have my brother and me join you. Obviously, there is something seriously amiss. But let's hear what your uncle has to say first." He walked Belle and Honey to the Farthingale carriage, the three of them silent as they were lost in their thoughts. He was the first to speak. "May I ride with you? I want to hear what your uncle has to say."

Belle nodded. "Yes, we brought you into this and don't want to keep anything important from you."

Their maid had been following a few steps behind them and must have been listening. She hopped up beside the driver, smiling at Finn as he helped her up. He then assisted Honey into the carriage but held Belle back a moment before lifting her up. "If things are as bad as we all fear, I think you both should stay in London with your aunt and uncle. Joshua and I will go to Oxford on our own to investigate."

Belle stared at him, looking ready to kick him in the shin. "Are you mad? We're not staying here when Father needs us."

He placed a restraining hand on her shoulder. "Your father *needs* you to be safe. I need you to be safe."

"Why? Because you're courting me?"

"Yes, and I don't want to see you hurt."

"Honey and I will be careful. Now that the family is aware of the danger, my father will have to tell us what is going on."

Finn hid his irritation. In truth, his heart was in his throat at the thought of Belle returning to her home. Anything could happen to her. Nor did he like her ability to dismiss him as though he meant nothing to her. "I'm going to marry you," he blurted.

"What?"

At least then, he could share her bed in order to protect her day and night from whatever danger lurked in Oxford. "I'm going to marry you."

She shook her head and laughed. "Now? At a time like this? No, you're not."

"I'm going to marry you whether you like it or not."

"Gad, was that a proposal? Because it sounded more like a threat than a declaration of love."

"Damn it, Belle. You're twisting my words again." He sighed. "I didn't mean it to come out that way. I'm worried about you. Not knowing what danger is lurking out there is gnawing at my gut. Let me protect you."

"Because I'm weak and cannot take care of myself?"

"No, because I'm in love with you and will go mad if I can't keep you safe." He understood she was overset about her father's injury. She was also unhappy about his own desire to marry her, but he knew his mind and was not going to deny his feelings for her.

Yes, he was arrogant and perhaps overbearing, but he loved her and did not like that she was dismissing him. She had just told him that kissing him would make her happy. A girl like Belle would not admit such a thing unless she returned his love.

Indeed, getting her to admit her feelings was like wrenching a sore tooth out of her mouth. Lots of pain, lots of resistance. "I will ask you to marry me again. I will ask you every day until you accept."

Her mouth dropped open. "Do you hear yourself? Are you serious?"

"Every day, Belle. Every single day."

"I'll pretend I didn't hear that last remark. Utter it again, and I shall discharge you from your assignment."

"You can't discharge me. You're not paying me to help. I'm offering it, and I'm damn well not letting you or your sister walk into the hands of these villains. Wherever you go, I follow. And before you shout at me and call me a possessive oaf, let me point out that I doubt Sophie or John will allow you to leave their home. If you somehow convince them to let you return to Oxford, they will insist on proper protection."

She frowned at him, no doubt peeved he was right.

"Joshua and I will provide it. And if you continue to protest..." He glanced up at the heavens. "Lord help me, I'll bring my mother along. She's Attila the Hun and Queen Boudica all rolled into one. She'll set Oxford in flames and chop off the heads of anyone who dares get near you."

Honey cast him a smile, for she'd been quietly listening to his and Belle's exchange. "Lady Miranda sounds lovely."

Finn ran a hand through his hair and gave a raspy laugh. "Actually, she is. You just don't want to get in her way when she's angry." He turned to Belle. "This is serious business. If you go home, I'm going with you. And I want to do it as your husband."

Belle climbed into the carriage and settled beside Honey with a huff.

Finn climbed in after her and sank his large frame onto the seat across from theirs. The Farthingale carriage had well-padded, black leather benches. It was a large and comfortable conveyance, able to accommodate a horde of Farthingales. "Marry me, Belle."

"I will not dignify that comment with an answer."

Honey cleared her throat. "Um, you might try that proposal as a question rather than a demand. I know you Braydens are military, and perhaps you've mistaken your intended wife for a soldier under your command, but..." She sighed and stopped talking since he and Belle were too busy frowning at each other to pay her any attention.

They hurried inside John and Sophie's home the moment the carriage rolled up to the front gate. The Farthingale butler, Pruitt, had been standing by the open door, obviously awaiting Belle and her sister. "Mr. Farthingale is in his study," he said, motioning to a solid mahogany door that was slightly ajar.

They all hurried in.

John had been pacing while Sophie was seated and wringing her hands. "Girls," she cried, jumping up and hurrying over to hug each of them. She paused to gaze at Finn uncertainly. John appeared relieved to see him, but obviously unsure how much to reveal.

"I happened to be passing by the Royal Academy when I saw your nieces rushing out. Is there anything I can do to help?"

Since Belle said nothing to encourage her uncle to confide in him, Honey took up the role. "Mr. Brayden knows everything we know, Uncle John." She glanced at Finn. "Belle and I sought his help. We were worried about Father. Something bad is going on, isn't it?"

John nodded. "Rupert sensed something was…off…the last time he visited Oxford. And now this sprained ankle. Only it's more than a mere sprain. Rupert thinks he was roughed up."

Belle and Honey gasped.

"Girls," Sophie said, obviously trying to remain calm, "tell us what you know."

Honey started the recounting, and Belle finished the story. "That's why I contacted Mr. Brayden," she said, casting Finn a weak smile. "We hoped to gain access to the business accounts this weekend. Now I'm worried we're too late. Mr. Brayden had volunteered to review them for us to try to detect the manner of fraud."

Her uncle ran a hand through his hair and cast Finn a wry smile. "We are much indebted to you, Mr. Brayden. I didn't think you'd want anything to do with Belle after…well, it doesn't bear mentioning."

Belle blushed. "Indeed, may we please forget that day and never think of it again? Mr. Brayden has been kind enough to forgive me. Let's move on. What's our next step? Do we know who is out to harm our father?"

"No. Rupert tried to get answers from him, but he refuses even to admit there is a problem. Your mother wouldn't talk to Rupert, either."

Honey sighed. "We're not surprised. They've been hiding the truth from us for months. This is why we asked Mr. Brayden to pretend to court Belle. We hoped our parents would not grow suspicious when we brought him home with us."

Sophie arched an eyebrow. "You're courting Belle?"

"No," Belle blurted. "Merely pretending."

Finn nodded. "Yes, I'm courting her." He crossed his arms over his chest and repeated, "Yes. She may be pretending. But I'm not."

Belle sank into one of the chairs beside her uncle's desk. "He doesn't mean it."

Finn wanted to throttle her.

Sophie moved to sit beside her. "Oh, my dear." She put her arm around Belle's shoulders. "These Braydens do not tiptoe around a subject. They say what they mean. Love can be frightening, especially when you've been raised to believe you are unlovable."

Belle glanced at Finn.

The urge to throttle her faded instantly, for all he saw was anguish in her fragile gaze. "I think," she said, taking a deep breath, "we ought to proceed with our plan. Honey and I will have our weekend party, and Finn and his brother will join us. How can we cancel, anyway? Holly, Dahlia, and Heather will be joining us, and they must have left York by now. There's no way to contact them and have them turn back." She glanced at Finn. "They're from the Yorkshire branch of Farthingales."

"You'll like our cousins," Honey said. "Holly is a widow, but her younger sisters are unmarried. They'll be staying in London with Uncle John and Aunt Sophie when Dahlia and Heather make their debuts next Season." She walked to her uncle's side to give him a quick hug. "You've been more than generous with all of us. This is why we feel just awful dragging you into this mess."

Belle agreed. "We'd hoped to handle it ourselves, but matters have become desperate, it seems. Do you think these villains would dare harm our mother?"

John's expression darkened. "I hope not. We don't even know who they are. Your father refused to tell Rupert anything."

Finn was more relieved than ever to have Joshua coming with him. They would engage a Bow Street runner or two to follow them. More precisely, the runners would be instructed to guard Belle and Honey. They were Farthingales. Independent. Headstrong. They would not sit quietly while he handled matters.

He had no doubt these sisters were going to dig into their father's affairs and turn over every rock until they found the snake who meant to harm him slithering beneath it. "We're scheduled to go up to Oxford the day after tomorrow. Joshua and I will ride over here first thing that morning and travel with the ladies."

Honey pursed her lips and frowned. "What if our father suspects your purpose and sends you away?"

Finn turned to Belle. "I'm not going to abandon you. There's a simple solution to the problem, and you know what it is."

"Marry you? Gad! You're insufferable." She wanted to throw a sofa cushion at his head, but her aunt had the good sense to cast her a warning frown before she could send it hurling at him.

He supposed he was being insufferable, but he didn't know how else to protect her. He knew he'd botched his marriage proposal again. Why couldn't he get it right? Dealing with financial matters was so much easier than dealing with Belle.

One did not have to lay one's heart open when reviewing a column of numbers.

He'd read the book. He'd talked to Tynan.

He'd listened and learned.

Or so he thought.

He wasn't an idiot.

What was he doing wrong?

CHAPTER EIGHT

BELLE WAS RELIEVED when Finn and Joshua chose to ride on horseback rather than join her, Hortensia, and Honey in the carriage as they traveled to Oxford. Of course, if given the choice, she and Honey would have chosen to ride horses rather than endure Hortensia's stern countenance. But it would not have been proper for them to travel in the company of young men without a chaperone.

Perhaps she was being too hard on Hortensia. After all, she'd been brought in on the problem and was as determined to help save her father as they all were.

As the carriage rolled out of London and sped up along the countryside, Belle looked out the window pretending to study the rolling hills and sheep-dotted meadows. In truth, her attention was on Finn. She knew she wasn't being fair to him. But she wasn't about to rush into a romantic entanglement. She'd been burned all her life by friends and then suitors who'd rushed off in fear after witnessing one of her attacks, treating her as though she carried a contagion.

Finn had witnessed one such attack. And yet, he spoke of marriage? It troubled her terribly. Men did not stay around long once they'd seen her in the throes and gasping for breath. Yes, Finn was more stubborn than most. In truth, more protective than most.

Perhaps this was the problem. He considered her helpless and unable to take care of herself. He'd anointed himself to the task of guarding her.

How long before he gave up in disgust?

And if she took him up on his offer and married him? She would become an onerous chore from which he could never escape. It might take watching her suffer through several episodes before he came to his senses and realized his mistake. Then the resentment would start to take hold. She'd see it in his eyes. She'd see it in his manner.

It would break her heart.

Indeed, she would shatter into a thousand pieces to see him hurt and regretful.

She cared for him too deeply to allow it, and perhaps she loved him.

This was something she refused to consider. He'd never leave her side if he knew how much she wanted and needed him. He had the Brayden sense of honor and duty. He lived by a code of chivalry straight out of medieval knighthood.

She refused to be a duty to him.

And what of his family? They would hate her for trapping him in an unwanted marriage.

No, she couldn't possibly marry him. But she would get her kiss and perhaps more…a touch, a taste of him. She would like to run her hands along his hard, muscled body, and if she mustered the courage to be naughty, put her lips to his warm skin and taste the salty heat of him.

Yes, that would make her happy.

They rode in silence for a while. Hortensia drifted off to sleep. A short time later, Honey sighed to gain her attention. "Belle," she whispered, "what do you think of Lord Wycke?"

"Lord Wycke?" She shook her head to bring her thoughts to the present. They had paid a call upon Lady Wycke the other day, and it had been pleasant enough. Her son, the Earl of Wycke, had made a brief appearance just as they were leaving. "I don't know. He seems nice enough. Why do you ask?"

"He invited us to a country weekend at his Cotswolds estate next month."

This surprised Belle. She had been so caught up in her own concerns she hadn't been paying attention to Honey. "Do you want to go? Or do you find him boorish?"

She laughed softly and shook her head. "I would call him reserved. Aloof. But never boorish. What do you think of him?"

"I liked him well enough. He has a bit of a rakish reputation, but he's very handsome, so I suppose women would find him hard to resist. He was quite good with his mother and seemed genuinely concerned for her health. I noticed she struggled finding her words occasionally." She inhaled lightly. "Honey, is there something you wish to tell me?"

"No. As you said, he has a bad reputation."

Belle rolled her eyes. "I didn't say bad. I said rakish."

"Isn't it the same thing?"

"No. Are you interested in him?"

"Not at all," she whispered with a dismissive shake of her head.

"How about Joshua Brayden?" Belle glanced out the window to the rider beside Finn. The brothers were of similar height and build, both big. Joshua's hair was more of a reddish-brown, much lighter than Finn's, which was almost black. "He's also quite handsome, and we know from Violet that all Brayden men are of good character. Violet glows like a little candle ever since meeting and marrying Romulus. She's incandescent. Do you think we'll ever fall in love like that?"

Honey pursed her lips in thought. "I like to think so, but who knows? Love is a precious gift, and true love is quite rare. As for me, I'm in no hurry to sacrifice the family business and my independence. I expect I will have to if I marry. He'd have to be awfully special for me to give it all up. Joshua Brayden seems very nice, but no. He's not the one for me."

"And Lord Wycke?"

"I don't see how he can have any interest in me."

Belle noted her sister had not ruled him out.

However, they dropped the conversation as their carriage drew up in front of their Oxford home. Belle loved the big, rambling manor that held so many happy memories for them. She gazed at its welcoming front door, and her heart began to flutter. "What will we do if Papa refuses to tell us the truth? Mama is just as bad. She's covering for him. I'm worried he'll destroy the accounts rather than risk us finding out what's wrong."

Honey nodded. "Let's not confront him immediately. Be jolly. Let's stick with our original plan for now. We're here for our house party, and we've invited friends and family to join us. Act concerned, but do not make too great a fuss if you see him limping. Pretend to accept whatever drivel he tells us. Most important, pretend you are in love with Finn, and that's why you've brought him home. You want him to meet your parents and gain their approval of his courtship."

Belle nodded.

Honey took her hand and gave it a light squeeze. "I know it isn't a pretense between you and Finn. Don't push him away because you think he's like the others. He isn't, Belle."

"I'll think about it." But to risk her heart just now was too much to ask. She'd give it more thought once they figured out what was going on with their business. By then, Finn would have enough of the messy affair and never bring up the topic of marriage again.

Honey shook Hortensia awake.

Their party was greeted at the front door by their elderly butler, Conyers. "Miss Honey. Miss Belle. It's so nice to have you back home. Your father could do with a bit of cheering."

Honey was much better at hiding her feelings. "Oh," she said with convincing sincerity. "Has something happened that we ought to know about, Conyers?"

The man glanced around uncertainly, no doubt cautious about speaking where others might hear. But Hortensia had been led upstairs immediately by the housekeeper. Finn and Joshua were seeing to the unloading of the luggage. Only she and Honey remained with Conyers at the moment. "Perhaps I spoke out of turn. But your father fell while at work and sprained his ankle. He's a bit banged up still. Your mother is most distressed. She's been walking around like a frightened bird ever since your father got hurt. Seeing her daughters again will lighten her spirit, I'm certain."

Belle was troubled when neither parent came downstairs to greet them. She knew they were at home and not at the shop. Conyers had added that bit of information before excusing himself to supervise the footmen who were carrying in their luggage.

"Mr. Brayden's bags go in the blue guestroom," he said, referring to Finn. "Captain Brayden's bags are to be placed next door to him in the green guest chamber." Joshua was in the army, so referring to him by his rank was an easy way to distinguish one brother from the other.

Belle wanted to ask Conyers more questions, but he was a loyal retainer and she did not wish to put him on the spot. Besides, she doubted he'd say more in front of Finn and Joshua, who had just marched in and were now standing beside them.

They all followed Conyers upstairs and waited while he efficiently saw to everyone being properly settled in their assigned chambers. Once they were alone in the hall, she and Honey pressed him for more information.

The look in his eyes was one of despair.

Honey sighed. "Conyers, tell us all you know. We're here to fix the problem. By the way, the Braydens are here to help us. You may tell them anything you would tell us."

"Yes, everything," Belle said for emphasis.

"Very good. I shall, but I wish there was more to tell. Whatever is going on concerns the shop. That's where you'll find the answers."

"What about the ledgers?" Belle asked. "Are they still kept here at home?"

He nodded. "Only your father has the key to the locked drawers. He carries it on his person at all times now. He stopped hiding it in the Chinese vase weeks ago. Probably realized we all knew about this not-so-secret hiding spot."

Belle cast him a warm smile. "You've been most helpful. We'll take it from here. Just let us know if you think of something else."

She and Honey exchanged glum glances as they watched their trusted butler stride downstairs. "Oh, dear," Honey said. "Seems we have our work cut out for us. How is Finn with picking locks?"

"I don't know. But he's quite perfect, isn't he? I'm sure he'll have a solution."

Honey's eyes widened. "Oho! So, you do like him."

"I am not discussing Finn Brayden with you." Belle gave her sister a quick kiss on the cheek and disappeared into her bedchamber to freshen up. "I'll be ready in five minutes. Meet you back out here."

The maid she and Honey shared was a cheerful girl by the name of Maggie. She knew their routines and preferences and had all in order by the time they were ready to return downstairs to the drawing room.

Belle wanted to go in search of her parents, but Honey held her back. "No, I'd like Finn to be with us when we first see them."

"Very well." Belle saw the wisdom in this. First impressions were often the most honest.

They did not have long to wait before Finn and Joshua joined them. Hortensia had decided to nap after the journey, so it was only the four of them awaiting her parents.

They weren't kept waiting long. Their father hobbled in, leaning on the arm of their mother.

Belle reached for Finn's hand, hardly aware of what she was doing.

She felt his fingers wrap around hers, imbuing her with warmth.

But she'd turned to him on instinct and quickly realized her mistake. She drew her hand away before her parents noticed and voiced their disapproval of the inappropriately affectionate display.

Tea was served after introductions were made, and they all sat down to engage in casual chatter. Belle sat close to Finn, purposely tossing him an adoring glance or two whenever she thought her parents were looking.

She did not want to overdo it.

He shot her an occasional steamy glance, and even though she expected it and knew it was part of their ruse, her body did not seem to understand this. Perhaps because his feelings were real, as he'd taken pains to tell her.

Her heart beat a little faster.

After enduring an inconsequential exchange of conversation about the weather, Belle decided to get to the heart of the matter. "Papa, we were hoping to show our friends the shop tomorrow morning. We'll go early, so we can be home by the time the other guests arrive."

Her father paled.

Her mother appeared ready to faint.

But her father recovered quickly. "No, my dear. It isn't a good idea just now. We have...repairs going on at the shop. You'd best stay clear of it."

"That's right." Her mother nodded a little too frantically. "All that dust, and who knows what else was stirred up by the construction? It isn't good for your lungs, Belle. No, indeed. You are too delicate. Stay away from the shop."

Belle wanted to press them on it, but Finn smoothly interceded. "Joshua and I went to university here. There are a few professors we'd like to see. Would you mind if we brought your daughters along?" He turned to Honey and Belle. "We'll take you for tea afterward. Or perhaps a picnic along the Isis?"

This was how locals often referred to the Thames where it coursed through Oxford. She glanced at Finn and wondered whether they'd ever crossed paths during his university days. It felt odd to think they might have.

Had she ever felt a little tug to her heart for no apparent reason while walking down one of the streets near their shop? Had her heart sensed his presence and awakened?

"Mr. Brayden," her father said, tossing Finn a knowing smile. "It has not escaped my notice that you seem quite attentive to one of my daughters."

Belle gasped. "Papa!"

Even though this was precisely the impression they'd meant to give, it was quite forward of her father to mention it here and now. "Our Honey is a lovely girl. You won't find one finer."

Honey choked on her tea. "Me? You think he's…"

Belle saw that her sister was angry enough to spit nails. Angry for her sake, but Belle took it all in stride. She was used to being ignored and overlooked, dismissed as the pitiful sister for all her life. "It's all right."

"No, it isn't." Honey set down her teacup, and her hands were now curled into fists at her sides. "What makes you think Mr. Brayden is interested in me?"

Belle tried to calm her sister. "Truly. It's all right, Honey."

But her sister was now blinking away tears. "No, it isn't."

Her parents ignored both of them, for they were too busy staring at Finn. He frowned back at them, obviously about to rise to Belle's defense, but a desperate shake of her head and the pleading in her eyes held him back.

He did not appear pleased but understood they were her parents, and she did not want him to interfere.

Their father turned to Joshua. "Captain Brayden," he said, studying Joshua, who was in uniform and cut a fine figure. He served in what he considered a 'bloody desk job' acting as army liaison to Parliament.

"Are you here to find yourself a wife as well? My three nieces will be arriving today, and I can assure you, they are all quite lovely."

Now, Belle was ready to burst into tears.

She knew they loved her, but it was painfully obvious they considered her unlovable to anyone else. "Father..." Her heart began to skip a little too wildly because she was overset. Finn had made her feel beautiful, but this was the harsh reality. No one could stay in love with her. "Father...you cannot..." She began to cough. How could he assume Finn cared for Honey? Or that Joshua couldn't possibly consider her. He'd offered up every Farthingale female of marriageable age except for her.

She was seated right in front of him. Was he that blind to her feelings? Her mother as well?

It doesn't matter. Finn cares for you.

But it *did* matter terribly. These were her parents. Yes, they had far more serious concerns, but it had always been this way. *Belle, you are the sickly one.* She was the daughter to be pitied. No one could possibly want her.

Yet, she was as much to blame. Isn't this exactly what she had been telling Finn? I'm no good for you. You'll end up disgusted with me.

She felt her lungs tightening.

No. No.

Then Finn took her in his arms and kissed her brow. Finn was the one whispering encouragement and words of love. "Yes, Mr. Farthingale. I am courting one of your daughters. It's Belle I love."

His words were like a soothing balm.

His hands held the touch of healing she needed to steady her erratic breaths. "Finn, you don't have to...say..."

"What? That I love you?" He did not appear to be uncomfortable uttering these words in front of everyone. "I've been an idiot, haven't I?"

She didn't know what he meant. "No, you've been...wonderful...to me."

"I proposed to you and never told you how I felt. Farthingales marry for love. So do Braydens. We were even reading that book Violet gave you on the meaning of love. And yet, this is the first time I've ever said it to you." He shook his head and sighed. "I didn't even tell you. I told your parents. I'm so sorry, Belle. I've botched this again."

"You've already proposed to my daughter?" Her father looked incredulous. He struggled to his feet. "To my daughter, Bluebell?"

Finn grinned at her. "Bluebell? Of course, all you Farthingales have flower names. I should have guessed." He gave her arm a squeeze before she got upset again and responded to her father. "If *marry me, Belle* counts as a proposal, then yes. I have offered to marry your Bluebell."

Her mother ran to her side and took her out of Finn's arms to hug her. "Oh, my dear! We are so happy for you. We never...but it has happened. And now we shall plan a lovely wedding."

Belle did not know why she was feeling so contrary, but she wanted to put a halt to any talk of weddings right now. Bluebell, indeed! And Finn was taking far too much pleasure in the knowledge of her given name.

"Bluebell," he whispered, and she might have been more irritated if his smile wasn't so affectionate.

But they needed to be free to go about Oxford looking for the villain who had hurt her father and was attempting to ruin his business, perhaps steal everything from him. They simply didn't know enough yet to understand what was going on. "No wedding plans, Mama."

She glanced at Finn, hoping he understood her purpose. If she agreed to marry him now, the entire week would be spent shopping for a trousseau and making arrangements for a grand wedding breakfast. They'd have no time to themselves to investigate. "Mr. Brayden has proposed to me, but I have not yet accepted him."

To her relief, Finn did not appear at all put out. He understood her reasons, which had nothing to do with her not loving him. She loved him deeply, and he had to see it reflected in her eyes. It did not matter that he'd revealed his feelings to her parents first. All that mattered were the words, *I love your daughter.*

Love.

She would find a quiet moment to tell him she felt the same.

As the tension began to mount in the room, her parents obviously shocked and displeased to learn she had not accepted Finn yet, Joshua silenced them all by rising and clearing his throat. "I have a very important question."

Her father frowned. "About why Belle is stubbornly refusing your brother's offer?"

Joshua grinned. "Well, my brother can be an insufferable arse at times. I can certainly attest to that."

Finn sighed. "What's your question?"

He winked at Belle. "We know your given name is Bluebell. But what is your sister's given name?"

Honey gasped. "Don't you dare tell him!"

Joshua was not to be denied. "Honeycomb? Honeybear? Honeysuckle?" His gaze traveled back and forth between the sisters. "Oh, lord. They named you Honeysuckle? Damn it. Now I owe Lord Wycke twenty pounds"

It was Belle's turn to gasp. "The two of you placed bets on my sister?"

Joshua held up his hands in surrender. "No...we...well, yes. But it isn't as bad as it sounds. We didn't...it was a friendly wager..."

Their father frowned. "Who is Lord Wycke?"

"No one important," Honey snapped back. "Just an earl who's about to die a slow and agonizingly painful death."

CHAPTER NINE

B ELLE AND HONEY had traveled to Oxford in the carriage loaned to
them by their Uncle John. The ever-reliable Abner Mayhew was
their driver who would return them to London by the end of the
week. Since they had the use of the carriage until then, Belle and her
sister, and Finn and his brother, hopped in it the next morning. They
told her parents they were going to visit Magdalen College, the school
Finn had attended while at university. However, it was merely a
pretext for spending the day in town to investigate what was really
going on at their perfume shop.

Hortensia had agreed to keep their parents occupied at home. She
was not pleased Belle and Honey were going about town in the
company of the two Brayden brothers, but this was not London, and
the rules were a bit more relaxed here. In addition, now that Finn's
intentions were known to be serious, there was less concern about
appearances.

No doubt her parents hoped Joshua and Honey being thrown
together would ignite a spark between them, but Belle had to admit
she saw none. They were polite to each other and chatted amiably, but
she knew Honey very well and saw no brightening in her eyes or light
intake of breath whenever his name was mentioned.

Honey had spoken of Lord Wycke on the ride up here.

Was he the one?

Belle did not feel too badly for Joshua. He was quite dashing and considered an excellent catch. Perhaps one of her cousins would strike his fancy. Holly, Dahlia, and Heather were due to arrive later today.

She shook out of the thought. Her mind ought to be on their shop and the troubles going on there, not on matchmaking. Besides, Honey was frowning at the two Braydens who were grinning back at her. "If either of you ever dare to call me Honeysuckle or reveal my given name to anyone, I shall carve you into little pieces with the very large, very sharply honed claymore that hangs over our drawing room hearth. Got it?"

Finn and Joshua chuckled.

"Got it," Finn said. "We give you our oaths. Right, Joshua?"

His brother nodded. "You have my word. I have no desire to be chopped up like overly ripe cabbage and fed to the hogs."

The sun was shining, and the blue sky was dotted with puffs of white clouds as the four of them descended the carriage in front of Magdalen College. Belle liked the way Finn's hands lingered at her waist as he helped her down. But they had much to accomplish today, and she could not afford to be distracted. "Abner, we plan to spend the day walking around the college. We'll stop at the Ramsford Tea Shop afterward. Will you pick us up there at three o'clock? That ought to give us time to return home and freshen up before our other guests arrive."

"As ye wish, Miss Belle."

They all watched Abner drive off.

Belle assumed they would walk directly to their perfume shop, but Finn led her toward the college. "Let's take a moment here first. We'll visit one of my old professors and then head to the shopping district. We told your parents this was our plan, and I'd like it not to be an outright lie."

So, they walked through the gate and met several of Finn's professors. They appeared delighted to see him. "My brother may look like a fool, but he's actually quite smart," Joshua jested. "He graduated with honors."

"And you?" Honey asked.

"Oh, I was sent down. The Oxford dons were quite disappointed in me, especially so soon after having my brother." He shrugged. "Scholarly pursuits are not my strength. I attended Balliol College while here, but I preferred pursuing a career in the military. The army is where I belonged. Defending England. It's a proud Brayden tradition."

"You must have some intelligence if you were assigned as army liaison to Parliament," Belle said. "Or does it only require you to have unlimited patience when dealing with the House of Commons and House of Lords?"

He laughed. "Aye, patience is a virtue. Also having a thick hide and an iron stomach for things can get mighty unpleasant in the bowels of government."

They spent the hour touring the college and its beautiful chapel and grounds before heading to the Farthingale shop. Belle could not hold down her excitement. This was her haunt, her domain where she reigned supreme. Well, her nose reigned supreme, but this was no time to quibble. She'd missed working in the back room and missed the bustle of shoppers coming in and out its attractive front door.

The shop was a free-standing building, a charming structure of whitewashed stone with bright, yellow trim and a large window in the front with artful displays to attract customers. The door was an invitingly warm, sunshine yellow. The display cases inside the shop were mostly of glass and maintained to a high polish. The perfume bottles were designed by their cousin, Rose, who ran one of England's finest pottery and glassware enterprises. The bottles were of delicate glass and were works of art in themselves, beautiful enough to rival the Italian Murano glass works in Venice.

Filling those bottles with scents to match the elegance of the glass was Belle's responsibility. She couldn't wait to show her work to Finn.

They had yet to step inside, but it did not appear any construction was taking place in or around the shop.

"Oh, Finn. There's no repair work going on here. Something is terribly wrong. Why do our parents want to keep us away?"

"I don't know. How about you and Honey go browse in the haberdasher's across the street while Joshua and I scout out your shop?"

She didn't like the idea at all. "You won't know what to look for. Honey and I would know immediately if anything seemed out of place. I think we should all go in."

Finn glanced at his brother.

Joshua ran a hand through his hair in consternation. "She's right, Finn. We'll be there to protect them if we run into trouble."

"Thank you, Joshua." Belle took her sister's hand and strode into the shop.

She and Honey had always gotten on well with the staff, but it seemed no one was happy to see them. Their head clerk, an older lady with gray-streaked hair by the name of Mrs. Wynne, scrambled down from a small ladder she'd been standing on to reach the upper display shelves. "Miss Belle! Miss Honey!" she said in an urgent whisper, fretfully glancing around. "You shouldn't be here."

"Why not, Mrs. Wynne?" Belle exchanged a worried glance with Honey. "What is going on? The air is so thick in here, you can cut it with a knife. Please tell us what's been happening. And don't pretend nothing has. It's obvious—"

She noticed a rather unpleasant-looking man come out from the back. He wore elegant clothes, but there was nothing elegant in his looks or manner. He was big and bulky and had a jowly, scarred face that had obviously been on the receiving end of several vicious street fights. She did not like the way he was smiling at her. "You're the daughter with the nose," he said, his gaze avidly fixed on Belle.

"We all have noses," Honey shot back. "Who are you, and what are you doing in my sister's laboratory?"

"Ah, and you're the fiery one. The one they call Honeysuckle." His expression turned lewd. "Come closer, sweetheart. I'd like to suckle–"

Finn and Joshua picked the man up as though he weighed no more than a child and tossed him out the front door. "Don't ever show your face here again," Finn said. "Touch either one of these young ladies and you're a dead man."

The man's face was red with rage as he picked himself up off the street and dusted himself off. "You'll regret this, you stupid London toffs."

He appeared about to reach into his jacket, but Finn and Joshua reached into their boots and withdrew their pistols, aiming them straight at his chest. Finn emitted a low, predatory growl. "You were saying?"

The villain raised his arms and silently backed away, scurrying out of sight as fast as his legs would carry his portly frame.

Belle rested a hand over her heart to still the hurried beats.

Finn noticed. "Belle, are you all right? I'm sorry if we frightened you."

She shook her head. "I'm fine." But she turned to Mrs. Wynne. "Who is that man? What is his business with our shop?"

"Oh, Miss Belle! Your father will send me packing if I tell you. Not that I know anything, only…there are some bad dealings going on."

"You're here all the time," Belle said, trying not to sound impatient. "Surely, you've overheard conversations. What did he and my father discuss?"

"Please, Mrs. Wynne," Finn said. "I can't protect Belle or Honey if I don't have the information. I know Mr. Farthingale believes their remaining ignorant will protect them, but after this encounter, you know it will only place them in greater danger. It is obvious the man intends to harm them. Who is he? Do you know if he's merely a lackey or the one running the operation?"

She glanced around nervously at the other clerks in the store. They all looked scared. She sighed, and after a moment, nodded. "His name is Mr. Runyon. He works for someone, but we don't know who. Someone powerful, or with powerful connections here in Oxford. I think the trouble started with your uncle."

"My mother's brother, Jacob Ewell," Belle said, turning to Finn and Joshua to explain. "He's my father's partner in the business."

Honey frowned. "He's also a gambler. Our parents have tried to hide this from us, but we know he has a serious problem. This could be how the trouble started."

Finn turned to Mrs. Wynne. "Did their uncle lose his share of the business to this unknown, powerful man?"

She nodded. "I'm fairly certain of it."

"And how often does this Mr. Runyon come around to collect what's due from Mr. Ewell?"

The woman's eyes began to tear. "At least once a week. But he's also taking from Mr. Farthingale now."

"Oh, dear heaven." Belle's hand went to her heart again. "Everything they've worked so hard to build up is now lost to some unknown snake? He means to chase my father out of the business and own it for himself, doesn't he?"

Mrs. Wynne's eyes were now tearing. "Yes, Miss Belle. I think he does."

Finn put an arm around Belle's slumped shoulders. "I hope that's all he intends."

"All?" She stared up at him in surprise. "Isn't it enough?"

"Not for him. The business isn't worth much without you. You're the *nose,* and that's why the Runyon chap referred to you this way when meeting you."

Belle cast him an imploring look. "What can we do, Finn?"

He rubbed his hand along the nape of his neck. "I don't know yet. Let me and Joshua do a little more investigating. I want to find out as much as we can about this Runyon fellow. I'll have my Bow Street runners work on it. I already have them following him. Hopefully, he'll lead them straight back to his employer."

Honey's eyes widened. "But how can your runners possibly do anything? We didn't know the man existed until a few minutes ago. They'll never find him in a city this size."

Finn glanced at Joshua, who gave him an almost imperceptible nod. "Tell them, Finn."

Belle looked at him. "Tell us what?"

"I brought two runners with me from London. They followed us up here and have been guarding you and Honey since we left your home this morning. They were standing on the corner when we tossed that vermin into the street. I only needed to motion to them, and they knew what I wanted them to do."

Honey shook her head and gave a wistful laugh. "You come prepared, don't you? I like that. When they return, will you introduce us to the runners? We ought to know their faces, so we don't mistake them for Runyon's scoundrels and accidentally shoot them."

"I will." He took Mrs. Wynne's hand and bowed over it. "I know I am asking much of you and your clerks, but please go on about your business as though we were never here. If pressed, stall as long as you can before letting on to Mr. Farthingale or Mr. Ewell that we were ever in the shop."

"Yes, my lord," she said, blushing.

Finn was not of the nobility, but none of them bothered to correct her mistake. Finn was noble in Belle's eyes. There was no one finer than him.

Belle glanced around the shop, relieved to see nothing had changed up front. But what of the back rooms? "May we stay a little while longer?"

Now that they were here, she wanted to show Finn her laboratory and needed to make certain this Runyon character had not tampered with any of her fragrances.

"I suppose it's all right. Whatever harm has already been done. But be quick, Belle. I don't want us here if Runyon returns. He won't come alone, and he'll be better armed."

While Belle entered her workshop with Finn, her sister and Joshua went into their father's office with Mrs. Wynne to review the daily accounts.

Belle hadn't been in the back room in several months, not since she and Honey had been sent to London to find themselves husbands. But no one would have touched her bottles or her notes. The staff had strict orders not to come in here or move anything around.

Upon closer inspection, Belle breathed a sigh of relief. The bottles were all in order, and only a couple of them looked as though they had been tampered with. She could tell from the lack of dust settled on those few bottles.

She pried open the three bottles that appeared to have been touched and inhaled the scent contained within. "They've been opened but not damaged."

"Let me smell them," Finn said, obviously curious. "Mmm, nice."

Belle smiled at him, liking his earnest curiosity. "Can you guess what's in them?"

Finn laughed. "No, not a clue. You're the expert. But they do smell nice. Just like you. What scent are you wearing today?" Since he was standing slightly behind her, he merely leaned forward, took a deep breath, and nuzzled her neck. "Oh, this one's nice. Belle, I like this one very much."

His lips were now on her neck, and the touch of them felt exquisite. She closed her eyes and leaned back as he circled his arms around her, continuing to nuzzle away.

"Really, Belle. Lord, have mercy." He moved to the other side of her neck. "I'm going to eat you up, you smell so good. What is that scent?"

Laughing, she twisted slightly in his arms to glance up at him.

"You're jesting, aren't you? Are you flirting with me?"

He appeared confused. "No. *The Book of Love* had an entire chapter on scent. It's one of the senses. Remember what we read first? To arouse a man's senses in a favorable way. So, are you going to tell me what scent you're wearing, or will we be here forever while I try to guess? Needless to say, I'm favorably aroused."

"You are?" She laughed again. "Well, thank you. But it's just me, Finn. No scent. Just my body. Well, I suppose I did use an oatmeal soap to wash this morning."

He paused in mid-nuzzle and turned her around to face him. "Hen's teeth. You're serious?"

She nodded. "What's wrong with you?"

He grinned and wouldn't stop grinning at her.

She rolled her eyes. "Honestly, Finn. What is so funny?"

"Not funny at all. Quite alarming, actually. But in a very pleasant way. The scent of you, Belle. I just experienced the scent of love."

"The scent of love?" She rolled her eyes. "Oh, for pity's sake."

"I'm serious. This is what the book says, that appealing to my senses is what matters for us to form our bonds of affection. You don't have to be beautiful to others, only to me. Your voice or appearance doesn't have to enchant others, only me. Others do not have to find your scent intoxicating."

"Only you do?"

"Yes, the only thing that matters is what I think of you. Obviously, the same for you. My scent, my looks. My voice. Do I make you swoon, Belle?" His smile turned devastatingly tender. "You know how I feel about you."

Yes, he had her in raptures.

He had her swooning and her heart in mad, wild flutters. "Stop distracting me, and let's have a look at my notes. I think someone's tried to read through them. Not that it would have done a thief or spy any good. I write my notes in a code that only Honey and I are able to decipher."

Finn's eyes rounded in surprise. "Well done, Belle. I'm impressed."

"Our business is cutthroat. I couldn't risk competitors getting their hands on my formulas. But I never expected the danger to come from within. I'm especially glad Mr. Runyon could not make sense of my code."

Finn's smile faded. "It's good for your business, but not for you. This is why his employer needs you. He wants those formulas."

She regarded him, appalled. "I'll never give them up!"

He took her by the shoulders and turned her to face him once more. "And if he threatens harm to someone you love? Honey or your parents?"

She gasped. "Oh, Finn. Do you think he'd dare?" But she knew the answer and responded to her own question. "Of course, he would. We simply must put a stop to his plans."

"We will, love." He kissed her lightly on the lips. "Braydens were born for this."

"Protecting the weak and helpless?"

"Belle, you aren't weak. You are brilliant. Just look at all you've achieved. As for helpless, I'm not sure about that either. I've heard stories about John and Sophie's daughters. How Lily outsmarted her abductors, and Daffodil saved the Duke of Edgeware. How did she not dislocate her shoulder shooting off an elephant gun? All of them, including Daisy, Laurel, and Rose, showed outstanding bravery. And need I say that your cousin Violet saved my life?"

Her eyes widened as she stared at his shoulder, at the spot he'd been wounded when Violet's so-called friends attempted to steal the donations from her charity recital and shot Finn when he tried to stop them. "Oh, Finn! This just proves how dangerous loving a Farthingale can be!"

He caressed her cheek. "Life is dangerous. No one knows what the future will hold. But what I do know is that the Farthingale women are as valiant as any decorated war hero. I think you are no different from the other women in your family. If put to the test, you'll use your wits to prevail. Only, I hope you are never put in that position."

"Did you call me *love*?"

"About five minutes ago. I didn't think you'd noticed." He laughingly groaned. "Is this all you got from my pretty speech?"

"No, I heard it all." She smiled at him. "Finn, I—"

Her declaration was interrupted when Honey and Joshua rushed in. "Uncle Jacob just walked into the shop. Quick! He can't find us here. Let's slip out the back way."

Finn took hold of her hand as they kept low and did not stop running until they'd turned the corner and were safely out of sight of the shop.

Finn immediately drew Belle into his arms. "Are you all right?"

Since she was not out of breath in any dangerous way, she hastened to assure him. "I'm fine. But thirsty. Let's discuss what we've found out over tea and cakes."

She eased out of his embrace with great reluctance, and the four of them walked briskly down the High Street, turning off onto a quaint side street near Merton College where the Ramsford Tea Shop was located. The place was not crowded yet, so they chose a corner table to lend them some privacy, and after ordering lemon cakes and tea, they settled down to business.

Honey spoke first. "Yesterday's receipts were quite good, Belle. The perfume shop turns a handsome profit, just as it has steadily done these past few years. The receipts from our other shops are delivered there at the end of each day. We've checked those as well."

"They're quite healthy," Joshua said.

Honey nodded in agreement. "Even if Father shared the earnings with Uncle Jacob—and now that horrid Mr. Runyan or whoever he works for—he should not be in financial distress. There must be something more going on."

"They've gone through all my formulas," Belle said, taking her turn to report her findings. "It is obvious they haven't managed to decipher them yet. The fragrances are untouched, save for a few, but they've not been tampered with."

Joshua set down his teacup. "Decipher them? Have you put your formulas in a special code?"

Belle nodded. "Only Honey and I know the key to solving it."

His eyes brightened. "Obviously, you're good at creating ciphers if no one has been able to figure yours out after an entire summer. But can you solve one you haven't created?"

Belle glanced at her sister before turning back to Joshua. "I think so. We all can. That is, me and my sister and our cousins. You'll meet Holly and her sisters later today. This is how we amused ourselves as children, by creating codes and then competing against each other to solve them."

Joshua was obviously intrigued. "Here's a riddle for you, and let's see if you can guess the answer. What word contains three double letters all in a row?"

Belle turned to her sister. "Do you know it, Honey?"

She nodded. "How about you?"

Belle nodded. "Let's give him the answer together. On the count of three. One...two...three."

"Bookkeeper," they both said in the same breath.

Joshua's eyes widened. "Well, I'll be damned. Yes, that's it."

Finn laughed. "Looks like the army's just found itself some new code breakers."

His brother nodded. "I'll keep you Farthingales in mind next time the matter comes up. How are you at languages?"

Belle swallowed her bite of lemon cake. "Only Latin, French, and Italian. But may we get back to the matter of who is stealing from our family business? I expect it is Runyon's employer, of course. Discovering his identity won't be too difficult now that Runyon has probably led your men straight to him."

Honey took a sip of her tea and nursed the cup in her hands. "And we know he's taken over Uncle Jacob's share of the business, no doubt to settle a gambling debt. It's Father's share that has me puzzled. It is obvious our father is paying this man out of his share as well. But why?"

Belle had just eaten the last of her cake, quickly swallowing it in order to continue her sister's musings. "Our father is not a gambler."

Finn regarded her thoughtfully. "Perhaps your uncle is still deep in the hole and has not paid off his vowels to Runyon's employer. Or…is it possible he is holding a secret over your father?"

Belle shook her head vehemently. "No, what secret can he possibly have? He's a happily married family man. How can you suggest such a thing?"

"I'm just thinking aloud, not making any accusations. He keeps his important papers in the locked drawers of his desk. The answer is likely hidden in there. Let's make it a priority. We'll search his desk thoroughly tonight, before he has the chance to move those records to another hiding place or destroy them."

The others nodded.

"Joshua and I will sneak down there after midnight, once we're certain everyone's asleep."

"Honey and I will join you. We ought to be the ones sorting through his papers while you men stand guard."

Finn did not like the idea. "Four of us, Belle? We may as well invite a herd of elephants to join us. We'll never make it downstairs quietly. Leave it to my brother and me. Isn't this what you invited us here to do?"

She nodded. "But, I did not mean for Honey and me to sit back and do nothing."

"You can help by keeping everyone distracted and away from the study while we're searching. I'm sure they'll all be asleep, but no one will suspect if you and Honey watch the hall and delay anyone who gets too close."

"What about your Bow Street runners? Will they come to the house? Father will know we're on to him if they show up on our doorstep."

"They won't. Their duty is to keep watch and follow you whenever you leave the house."

"How do you communicate with them?" Belle was curious to know how they provided information to Finn.

Joshua leaned forward to address them quietly when a party of students entered and sat at the table next to them. "Finn and I will meet our *friends* right after supper. It won't take long to exchange what we've learned and formulate new plans. We'll only be gone an hour."

"In the meantime, both of you stay with your family. Don't go off by yourselves for any reason. If you are being watched by Runyon, you'll be safest remaining together and in the company of others. Who else besides your Yorkshire cousins will be arriving today?"

"Some friends of my parents," Belle said. "But this assumes they've made good time from Cornwall. It isn't safe to travel after dark, and they'll need to rest their horses. They might stop at an inn for the evening and arrive first thing in the morning. More guests will arrive tomorrow for our garden party, but most of them are local and won't be staying overnight."

Finn pursed his lips. "Let's hope their friends don't make it here this evening. The fewer people wandering the halls, the better."

Belle finished the last of her tea just as the proprietor advised them their carriage had arrived. She was about to rise when struck by an unpleasant notion. "Do you think Runyon will be invited?"

Honey stared at her. "Oh, goodness. I hope not. He's a horrid man and a lout. If he does show up, then it will prove he has a tight hold on the business."

"He won't be invited," Finn muttered. "He'd stick out like a sore thumb. But his employer won't be so obvious to recognize. That's who we ought to be looking out for. He's the real danger. He's the one with the stranglehold on your parents."

Belle's heart skipped a beat, for the problem was so much worse than she had ever considered. Finn had warned of this. He'd sensed the greater danger all along. Why couldn't it have been simple, merely a matter of an employee skimming off the top? She was truly worried, more than she'd ever been in her life. She gazed at Finn. "What dark secret does this man hold over my family?"

CHAPTER TEN

FINN FELT THE heat of the afternoon sun on his shoulders as he stood on the front steps of Belle's home, his arms folded across his chest, watching Belle and her sister greet their cousins who had just arrived from Yorkshire. Joshua stood beside him, his arms also crossed over his chest, so they gave the appearance of matching bookends.

Perhaps they were a little more frightening than mere bookends, more like sentinels guarding the entrance to a forbidden city. "I wonder if they're as pretty as Belle and Honey," Joshua muttered. "Who can tell with those bloody garish bonnets they're wearing? Gad, just listen to them. They're all chattering at once. Can they even hear what the others are saying?"

Finn chuckled. "Yes, they seem capable of carrying on several conversations at once. Men tend to think in a straight line. I say *this*, and you respond with *that*. Women can follow several threads at the same time. And they also have the ability to know who you're referring to with merely the use of pronouns. He said. She said. We don't have a clue who *he* or *she* is, but they know and get it right every time."

Joshua shook his head and laughed.

Finn pressed on, for Joshua was the most serious of his brothers and rarely laughed. "Not only that, they can follow bloodlines with ease. My mother's brother's wife's uncle. My butcher's mother's neighbor's grandson. We're lost after the first connection, but these women get the entire chain right every time."

Joshua rolled his eyes. "Bollocks, you've been reading that stupid book, haven't you? And now you've gone and fallen in love with Belle. It's turned you soft in the head."

"Just wait until it's your turn."

"Hah! It won't ever be," Joshua insisted. "I'm too careful for that. No woman will ever use that book to cast her spell on me."

Finn shrugged. "Fine, be that way. For the record, I fell in love with Belle before I ever read the book."

"But she had just been given that book by Violet. Within the hour, Belle had cut you down at the knees, toppled you like a giant oak." He made the sound of a saw slicing through tree bark—*ee-ew, ee-ew*—and followed it with the sound of a crash.

"Josh, you're an arse."

He arched an eyebrow. "I love you, too. Even though you're a monumental bull's pizzle."

The breeze had calmed, as it often did at this time of the day, offering no respite from the unrelenting sun. The air was laden with moisture, although there was no hint of rain on the horizon. However badly Belle and Honey felt about the trouble at their shop, they were genuinely cheered to see their cousins.

There were hugs and kisses all around as the five cousins laughed and continued to chatter all at once. Belle introduced Dahlia, Heather, and Holly to Finn and Joshua.

When the ladies moved inside, he and Joshua held back. "Hen's teeth," Joshua muttered, "you owe me for this. Solving a mystery is one thing, but living in a barracks of women? I think my brain might burst."

"Stop whining. This isn't so different from our family gatherings. We Brayden boys don't hug or kiss each other—"

"No, we wrestle each other to the ground and see whose teeth will get knocked out first."

"None of us has lost teeth yet. The point is, we're happy to see each other. We just have a different way of showing it."

Joshua stared at one of the newly arrived ladies wearing an unflattering green bonnet. "So, what do you think? Holly or Hollyhocks?"

"What?"

Joshua slapped him on the shoulder. "I'm speaking of Belle's cousin. But you have eyes only for Belle. You haven't stopped gawking at her since we got here. You may not realize it, but other females do exist. I'm speaking of her cousin, Holly, the pretty one with sad eyes we were just introduced to. Do you think her name is simply Holly, or did her parent take the embarrassing step and name her Hollyhocks?"

Finn snorted. "I don't know. Why don't you find out?"

"I can't ask her that. It would be rude."

"Fine, so ask Belle or Honey." Finn returned the slap on the shoulder with a light, playful punch. "Or ask Hortensia, why don't you? She knows the entire Farthingale family history and will have a comment for all of it."

"She already tosses me the stink eye, and I haven't done anything to her precious nieces."

"Ah, but she knows you will." Finn arched an eyebrow and grinned wickedly. "We're depraved barbarians who have only one thing on our mind."

They strode inside and joined the ladies who had made it no farther than the entryway as they removed their bonnets, gloves, and travel capes. Joshua appeared to have stopped breathing, but Finn paid little attention to his brother. His gaze was now trained on Belle, his heart tugging at the smile on her face and the glow in her eyes. He wanted her to look at him the same way.

With love and happiness.

She was getting there but hadn't allowed herself to trust her feelings yet.

While Conyers retreated to put away the bonnets and capes, Honey and his brother joined the new arrivals in the drawing room. To his surprise, Belle held him back. "You called me *love* earlier. Did you mean it, Finn?"

"Yes, Belle. I did."

"Thank you." She cast him a heart-melting smile before joining the others in the drawing room.

He followed, disappointed she hadn't returned the sentiment, but he was here for the week. Hopefully, she would trust herself enough to admit what was in her heart by the end of his stay.

The ladies soon retired upstairs to freshen up before supper. Because the Yorkshire cousins were tired from their journey, supper was earlier than usual and kept to a simple affair. A soup course, fish course, and a hearty lamb stew. The dessert course was rustic fare, comprised of strawberry tarts and an apple pie crumble.

Belle's parents were unusually quiet throughout the meal. Belle and Honey filled in as hostesses and did their best to keep the conversation light and constant. They specifically mentioned their tour of Magdalen College and the tea shop afterward. Finn could not tell whether Belle's parents had learned of their encounter with Runyon. He did not think so, but expected they would soon hear of it from that odious cur.

Therefore, it was most important to go through her father's papers tonight before he hid or destroyed documents of consequence.

He and Joshua made excuses about meeting old friends for a drink and departed for the heart of town immediately after supper. They were both eager to hear what the Bow Street runners had found out. These men had come highly recommended, and Finn expected they would be well worth their fee.

"I hope we did not keep you waiting too long, Mr. Barrow," Finn said, taking a seat beside the portly, older man at the Crow and Raven, a popular tavern frequented mostly by merchants and laborers. One did not find students or gentry drinking here.

"Not at all, Mr. Brayden. I was enjoying a pint. Following brigands is a thirsty job."

Joshua took the chair across from Homer Barrow. "What have you found out for us?"

Mr. Barrow took a hefty gulp of his ale and then set down his mug. "This Runyon fellow is a right cove, he is," Homer muttered. "Nasty piece of work. My colleague, Mick, and I followed him to a gaming hell. It's called the Pleasure Cave, but ye won't see a sign for it anywhere on the street. Indeed, on the outside, it looks like a pleasant, Upper Crust residence. This particular establishment services men of the better classes. Activities other than gaming take place there as well, if ye get my drift."

Finn nodded, for it was not uncommon for such a house to address all needs—drinking, gambling, whoring. Students were likely their best customers, young men with lustful desires and generous allowances with nowhere to slake their raging urges. This place was not so very old, for Finn had visited several such establishments when he was a student and would have heard of this one had it existed while he was at school. "Do you know who owns this gaming hell?"

"Not yet. But my friend Mick just got hired as a dealer. Apparently, there's a high-stakes card game taking place tonight, and their best dealer showed up injured."

Finn and Joshua exchanged glances. "You didn't do anything to…"

"The man? No, we don't operate that way…usually. Funny thing, though. The poor chap tripped on his way to work and broke his nose." He tapped on his bulbous red nose for emphasis. "Mick and I just happened to be close by and offered to help him out. We walked him around the corner to the gaming house since he appeared unsteady on his feet. To make a long story short, Mick's replacing him for the next two nights. Can't have a dealer with the face of a gargoyle staring at them well-heeled players. Anyway, Mick's very good with cards. They've hired me as a bartender for the night. Ye needn't worry. We'll have a name for ye by tomorrow."

"Thank you, Mr. Barrow." Finn was eager to get his hands on the brigand who was trying to ruin Belle's family. "How are you set for funds?"

He cast Finn a jowly grin. "No complaints. We're fine. Besides, pay's good at the Pleasure Cave. We have all we need for now."

After making arrangements to meet Mr. Barrow tomorrow morning by the chapel at Magdalen College, he and his brother returned to Belle's house. The ladies were in the drawing room, Hortensia and Belle's mother having a glass of sherry, while the younger ladies were drinking lemonade.

He glanced around. "Where's Belle?"

"She just went upstairs to fetch a book she wanted to show us."

Joshua groaned. "That damn love book again."

Although he spoke in a whisper, Hortensia's ears perked, and she frowned at Finn's brother. "Drinking and cursing," she muttered, scowling in disapproval. "Is this what they train you for in the army, Captain Brayden?"

Honey and her cousins were struggling to suppress their chortles. Joshua was right. Hortensia was giving him the stink eye. Finn wasn't sure why. Joshua was a decent man, but you'd never guess it by the daggers the old harridan was tossing at him with her sour-prunes gaze.

Finn was just about to leave Joshua with the women—he was a trained soldier, battle-hardened—surely, he could deal with one old harpy and a bevy of beautiful young ladies while he went off in search of Belle.

He didn't like that she was alone, even for a moment.

Danger could be lurking anywhere in this house. One had only to look at her mother's ashen complexion and the defeated slump of her shoulders to know this family was in a bad way.

He'd just started up the steps when she appeared at the top of the landing, carrying the faded, red leather tome in her hands. She scurried downstairs toward him. "Finn, you're back!" She kept her voice low, in an urgent whisper, and took his hand when she reached his side to hastily lead him into the music room. "I hope no one saw us. What did you find out?"

"Not much. Mr. Barrow followed Runyon to a gaming hell. He's got a man placed on the inside now, dealing cards. He's managed to get himself in as a bartender. We hope to learn more tomorrow."

Belle regarded him curiously. "He's very resourceful. How did he manage that?"

Finn shrugged. "It's a long story, but this is his reputation. He gets things done. He finds a way into the enemy stronghold without arousing suspicion. Whoever is running the establishment is probably the man we're after. Likely, he's well-bred. Perhaps the disgraced son of a nobleman. He caters to an elegant crowd, knows how to treat them in the manner to which they are accustomed. Meaning he indulges them, even as he steals from them. I hope to have a name for him before tomorrow's garden party."

"Have you considered the person Runyon answers to is a woman? After all, what would a man want with perfume shops? He might want to smuggle the merchandise, but to be involved in selling it? Producing it?"

"You have a point, but it is unlikely that the Pleasure Cave is run by a woman."

"The Pleasure Cave?" Her eyes rounded in horror. "It sounds taw-dry."

"Because it is tawdry. More goes on than simply gambling. But that is neither here nor there. I won't discount that it might be a woman behind this shady gaming hell or the scheme to steal the business from your family. But profit is profit. Anyone of low moral character could be in charge, be it man or woman. Mr. Barrow will tell us more tomorrow."

"I suppose you're right."

"Meanwhile…" He lifted the book out of her hands and set it on a side table, then took her in his arms. "Belle, my heart shot into my throat when Joshua and I walked in and noticed you were missing. Don't underestimate these villains. They could be anywhere, even in your home."

"Lurking and waiting for the chance to steal me away? Because of my discerning nose?"

He didn't want her to make light of the matter. In truth, he wanted to take her away from Oxford and the danger ever-present here. "Don't jest about it, Belle. You mean a lot to me. I'd lose a part of my soul if anything ever happened to you."

She reached up on tiptoes and flung her arms around his neck. "I…I…oh, Finn. I'm hopeless. Thank you for believing in me the way you do." She kissed him with sweet, inexperienced ardor, pressing her soft lips to his and sighing into his mouth when he took over the lead.

He gentled the kiss, stroked his tongue along the seam of her lips to tease them open. His tongue slid inside her mouth, joining with hers, tangling and dipping in a timeless dance that she had yet to master. What she lacked in experience, she more than made up for in her demurely unrestrained response.

When he drew his lips off hers to kiss his way down her slender neck, she tried to speak again. He knew what she wanted to tell him, but she was struggling with the words. "That's delicious."

He felt the pillow of her breasts against his chest as she molded her body to his, tipping her head to the side, so he had free access to her neck. She felt so good against his body. Her touch, the taste of her skin.

He should have drawn away, for others would come looking for them soon. But he needed another moment to breathe her in, to soak in each sensation she aroused in him. He cupped her breast, liking how the soft, plush mound filled his palm. This felt so right. Why couldn't Belle understand it?

"Finn…"

He inhaled the heat of her skin and continued to trail kisses along her slender neck. "What is it you're trying to tell me, love?"

She gasped as he ran his thumb along the taut bud of her breast, but instead of drawing away, she arched her back and leaned into him. "Finn!" She spoke his name again in a soft, ragged whisper, giving him access to her other breast. "I want to say it back to you."

"You can, Belle. No one's stopping you." He understood what she was trying to tell him. He knew she loved him. It was never about her feelings for him. Her doubt sprang from distrust of her own worth.

Having seen the way her family treated her, he now knew why she had such a difficult time accepting romantic love. They loved her, of course. But they saw her as a wounded bird, too sickly and frail to be loved by anyone but themselves.

He wanted to carry her upstairs and make slow, endless love to her. He did not know what else to do to prove he'd always love her.

But that would be a discussion for another day. Tonight, he would be busy searching her father's study. Something important had to be hidden within those locked drawers. "It doesn't matter, Belle." Her skin tasted so sweet. Her body felt so soft and perfect. "The words will come in time. I know how you feel about me. I know I have your heart as you have mine."

She nodded. "You do have it, Finn. Every bit of it."

"Then everything will work out." But as he spoke, he felt a sudden sense of doom. He didn't know why this foreboding had come over him, but his senses never lied.

He tucked a few loose curls behind Belle's ears and forced a casual smile as he released her. "You're too tempting by far. We'll give your family quite a show if we stay here any longer."

"I think they could catch you down on bended knee with a ring or other love token in hand, and they still would not believe you wanted to marry me."

"I only care that you believe it." He watched as she smoothed her gown, knowing if he placed his hands on her, that gown would be unlaced in a trice and slipping off her body rather than staying on.

She smiled at him. "I'm starting to. You can be very persuasive."

He wanted to take her straight up to his bedchamber, damn the consequences. The worst that could happen is they'd be forced to marry.

He wanted nothing better than to marry Belle.

Of course, he wouldn't force her. She would come around to it on her own soon enough.

His feeling of foreboding returned.

Something bad was going to happen tonight, but what?

CHAPTER ELEVEN

THE CLOCK AT the top of the stairs chimed one o'clock in the morning as Finn and Joshua stealthily prowled downstairs to the study. Finn had made clear to Belle and her sister that he did not want them skulking around downstairs. Obviously, his wishes had fallen on deaf ears, for the study door was open, and two slender figures were outlined beside the large desk. He saw them in the slash of silver moonlight filtering in through the window.

"Damn it, Belle." He quietly shut the door and lit the candle he'd brought down with him. "What are you thinking? I told you and Honey that I didn't want you in here."

She smiled back at him. "You need us to make sense of whatever you find."

He wanted to be angry with her but simply couldn't summon more than mild irritation. He supposed she was right, and he was behaving like an overly protective oaf. He couldn't help it. She'd brought beauty into his life, and he wanted to hold on to the precious splendor of it forever.

"Not if it's ledgers, you don't." But he was losing this battle. Not even he felt strongly about this anymore. He couldn't send her away now that he'd seen her by candlelight. *Hen's teeth*. Did a prettier girl ever exist? She wore a light robe over her nightrail, and her long hair was in a loose tumble down her back. She looked exquisite. Adorable. Too good to be true. "I can read those for myself," he said, fighting to suppress the ache in his heart. Lord, he wanted to marry this girl.

Belle frowned. "There must be something other than ledgers hidden in here."

Honey nodded. "I'm sure we'll find something about Uncle Jacob's gambling debt. It must be bad if he's dragging our parents down along with him."

Sighing in surrender, Finn came around the desk and placed his candlestick atop it. No one said a word while he knelt beside the locked drawers and worked the metallic pick in the keyhole until he heard its soft click. "Got one open."

Joshua laughed. "I always knew there was larceny in you. Good to know you're not quite the saint we all believe you to be."

"A saint?" He glanced at Belle, tossing her a wink. "Little chance of that. Ah, there are papers in here. Take them out and start looking through them, ladies. I'll start on the other drawers. Joshua, stand by the door and alert us if you hear someone coming."

He lit another candle so that Belle and her sister had light to read by, for he still needed his own candle. It wasn't so much to pick the lock, for this was mostly done by feel. But he suspected there were hidden drawers within the desk or a false bottom within the drawers, and he needed light to find them.

He understood enough about human nature to know there were secrets one didn't want others to know because they might prove embarrassing, and then there were *secrets* no one else could ever know because they would destroy your life and those of your loved ones forever. These were the sort of secrets kept in hidden drawers.

He now suspected Belle's father had one of those destructive secrets.

He hoped he was wrong.

Was this the reason for his earlier sense of foreboding?

He shook out of the dreaded thought as he unlocked the second and third drawers with little difficulty. "Belle, there's more in here."

He lifted out a stack, setting the ledgers aside for his later perusal before handing her the correspondence and other documents mixed in with the ledgers.

Belle took them from him. "Oh, look. Honey, these are certificates of our birth. And this is the deed to our main shop. Finn, what are you doing?" She watched as he returned his attention to the empty drawers.

"Nothing. Just searching for a duplicate key." What he was actually seeking was a hidden cavity, but he could not let Belle or Honey know about it. If he did find one, he'd quietly review its contents, and if necessary, take its secrets to the grave.

Her eyes widened in surprise. "Why would he keep a duplicate key locked in his desk? Wouldn't it make more sense to keep it somewhere accessible?"

He glanced at her, wishing she would distract herself with the batch of papers he'd just handed her. "Yes, but perhaps it's a key to something else. It can't hurt to look. Does your father have a safe in here as well?"

"Behind his mother's portrait," Honey said. "But we don't know how to open it. Oh, but you are a man of many talents. Is breaking into safes one of them?"

Finn winced. "I hope so."

Joshua laughed softly. "And the saint tumbles farther down the ladder of perfection. Thank goodness."

"Shut up, you arse." But he chuckled as well. "Keep your eye on the door. Honey and Belle, can you take down that portrait of your grandmother? Or is it too heavy to manage?" He didn't really need them to do it but wanted to distract them as he dug into the hidden drawer.

Belle must have been watching him, for she suddenly rushed to his side. "What have you found?"

"Nothing."

Honey now joined her and gasped. "Is that a secret drawer?"

Blast. He ought to have waited and quietly come down here on his own later. "It isn't important. Go back to reviewing the other papers."

But neither sister budged. "There's something inside. Looks like an official document. And there's a newspaper clipping with it."

Belle peered over his shoulder, stopping him when he tried to shove the drawer closed. "What are you doing? This must be important. What can it be?"

Finn did not want either sister reading these papers before he had the opportunity for a first look. This was the *secret*, the one that could destroy lives. Their father had held it back from his own family for a reason. "Let me see it first."

Belle was still hovering over his shoulder. "Why?"

He muttered an oath under his breath, cursing himself again for his stupidity. He'd opened his big mouth, and now Belle and her sister knew these documents existed and were curious to learn what they contained. Even if he held them off this evening, how long before they crept down on their own and went through the contents?

"Bollocks!" Joshua suddenly yelped and hauled another body into the study.

"Damn it, what now?" Finn groaned.

Another Farthingale. The oldest cousin, Holly. Not that any of them were old. Although widowed, Holly could not have been more than four and twenty. Perhaps five and twenty at most. She was a handful in Joshua's arms, squirming and struggling as he held a hand over her mouth and had her pinned against his body while she tried to club him over the head with what appeared to be a candlestick. Or was it a fire iron?

Ouch! She landed a solid blow on Joshua's head. Good thing he had a stubborn, thick skull. Still, that was going to hurt.

"No, Holly! Stop! It's us. It's all right. Finn and Joshua are helping us out," Honey said, also keeping her voice to an urgent whisper.

As Honey's words finally penetrated, Holly stopped struggling.

Joshua released her with a groan and staggered into a chair, rubbing his head. "Christ Almighty! You pack a wallop."

"I'm so sorry." She went to Joshua's side. "What are you doing in here? I came down for a glass of milk and thought I heard an intruder."

Joshua frowned at her. "So, you decided to come in here and investigate on your own? What would you have done if I truly was an intruder? Or if there was a band of thieves in here? You should have run for help instead."

She pursed her lips and responded with a frown of her own. "It seems to me I was doing just fine. How badly did I hurt you? Oh, dear. You're bleeding. You'll have a nasty lump in the morning."

Finn came to his brother's side. Although they often joked and wrestled and punched each other, it was always done in good fun. But to see his brother seriously hurt...nothing else mattered at the moment than to have him tended to at once. "Josh, how bad is it?"

"I'll be all right. Sore, but I'll heal. She landed one good thwack to my head with whatever instrument of torture she was carrying."

"A candlestick," Holly said, her eyes now tearing. "You have a small cut where I struck you." She withdrew her handkerchief.

Honey ran to a side table where her father kept bottles of scotch, brandy, and other spirits. She grabbed the brandy. "Here, Holly. This will do to cleanse the wound. Will he need stitches?"

"No, it's just a tiny cut. Grit your teeth, Captain Brayden. This is going to burn." Holly soaked her handkerchief in brandy, paused a moment to allow him to prepare himself for the pain, then placed the brandy-soaked handkerchief to his head.

Joshua inhaled sharply. "Mother of– Ow! Were you Attila the Hun in an earlier life? Ow! Or a Spanish inquisitor? Gad, you're a lethal lass. Are you done yet?"

"Almost done." Holly set aside the handkerchief and began to inspect the rest of his head. He flinched every time she poked and prodded. "My goodness, is every man as big a baby as you?"

"Is every Farthingale female as bloodthirsty as you? I'm fine. Stop pawing me with your clumsy fingers."

As Joshua continued to grumble, Finn and Honey exchanged a grin in relief. The blow had not been a direct hit, but a glancing one. It left only a small cut. There would be a lump by morning, hopefully one that would subside quickly.

Finn resolved to stay by his brother's side for the rest of the evening. He could sit in his brother's chamber and watch over him while reading through the ledgers. It was an efficient use of his time since he had to remain awake all night to read these shop accounts anyway. He rose to return to the desk and stuff the damning contents back in the hidden drawer but realized he was too late. "Belle?"

While everyone had been hovering over his brother, Belle had stayed by the desk and picked up those secret documents. Her face was ashen even in the golden glow of candlelight. He noticed her hands were trembling. "Sit down, love," he said, taking the papers from her.

This was bad.

She sank into her father's chair and buried her head in her hands.

Finn quickly perused the newspaper clipping and the document contained with it. A marriage certificate between Constance Ewell—since Constance was Belle's mother's name, he assumed it was her—and a Matthew Fenton. This was dated twenty-six years ago. He then read the clipping, which appeared to be the obituary of one, Matthew Fenton, who died last year. *Believed drowned at sea twenty-four years ago. Returned to England one year ago.*

Blessed saints! This was worse than he ever imagined. He studied the marriage certificate and the clipping, hoping he'd made a mistake. But the truth stared him in the face. Constance, believing her first husband to be dead, had married Edgar Farthingale and given birth to their two daughters, Honey and Belle. This had been a second marriage for Constance. A bigamous marriage because Matthew

Fenton had been alive until a year ago. Which meant Honey and Belle were illegitimate offspring.

Finn knelt beside Belle and took her hands in his. Still, she would not look at him. "Belle, it makes no difference to me. It's you I want, not some stupid piece of paper."

"But it matters. When word gets out, no one will want to have anything to do with Honey and me."

He lifted her out of the chair and wrapped her in his arms. "I've just told you, I don't care. Once you and I are married, no one will care."

Her eyes were filled with pain as she finally met his gaze. "You must care. How can you not? Attaching yourself to me would ruin your sterling reputation. I'd destroy in a single day all you've worked so hard to achieve."

"Belle, I make people money. Yes, they may shun us in public for a few months until the next scandal comes along. Who gives a damn? But at the end of the day, they'll still seek out my advice. My family and yours will never shun you. I'm well connected. Indeed, so are you. The only possible way you can ruin my life is by *not* marrying me."

Honey came to their side and took a moment to read the marriage certificate and news clipping. "Oh, dear."

Finn noticed her legs begin to buckle and took her in the circle of his arms along with Belle. He held the two sisters as they began to cry. "Listen to me, both of you. This will all work out. The Farthingales and Braydens will protect you. This is what families do for each other. Honey, you will come through this. I promise you."

"It's all right, Finn. Don't make promises you know you can't keep. Marry my sister, and do it as soon as possible."

"No, Honey! How can you goad him to act so foolishly?"

"It isn't foolish." She sighed and turned to Finn. "Belle is stubborn. It will take persistence and determination to convince her this is the right choice. As for me, I wasn't keen on marrying anyway. But I may have to come live with you and Belle if we can't save the business, and the family is left penniless. I'm sorry to be a burden—"

"You'll never be a burden," Finn said. "We'll sort through this mess."

Finn turned to his brother.

Joshua nodded. "You have my oath, I won't breathe a word of this to anyone."

Holly was wringing her hands. "Nor will I, not even to my sisters. Captain Brayden, we'd best leave them now. Your brother and my cousins will confide in us further if they think we can help. Otherwise, it's none of our business."

She helped him up and propped her shoulder under his arm to keep him balanced, for Joshua, despite earlier assurances he was fine, did not appear all that steady on his feet. Perhaps he was playing it up a bit because he enjoyed Holly's tender ministrations. Finn couldn't worry about his brother just now. He ran a hand through his hair in consternation and studied the two distraught sisters. He sat them down, his attention particularly on Belle for fear this unwanted news would bring on a breathing attack.

Although her breaths were erratic, it was only from crying, and she appeared otherwise composed. "Belle, I mean it. This doesn't change my feelings for you. I offered for you before, and I'm offering again. I want to marry you. Not out of pity."

She looked up at him with tearful eyes. "Out of what then?"

"Out of sheer selfishness. I want you by my side always. I want you to be my wife, and I don't want any other man to have you. I also happen to love you. If you love me, then you'll understand what I mean when I say that I can't be without you. It's as simple as that."

She nodded. "I do know."

"Then let's not wait. I'll obtain a special license, and we can be married before the week is out."

"No, Finn. This is your protective instinct on fire just now. Let's see what happens over the course of this week. There's still plenty for us to do. As it is, we'll have to confront my parents, but let's hold off until after the garden party. I want them to enjoy their friends and not feel ashamed."

Honey agreed. "We'll have to keep them out of the study somehow. Father will know something is wrong at once since we can't lock the drawers without a key. Even if we could manage to lock these drawers, I'm sure he'll notice his papers have been shuffled around."

Belle groaned. "No wonder they've been acting so strangely these last few months. That must have been when they learned Matthew Fenton was alive."

"What a horrible man," Honey muttered. "He could have had the good grace to remain dead. I wonder if Mama loved him."

"It doesn't much matter, does it?" Belle mused. "She made a new life with our father and never saw him again...or...perhaps she did, and they all tried to keep it quiet. I don't know."

Finn took her hand and gave it a light squeeze. "It does no good to think about it now. We'll discuss it with your parents after the party. For now, let's go through the ledgers and papers just as we planned and see what else we can discover. Never mind about the safe for now. I think these documents were the important ones your father was desperate to protect."

Honey nodded. "The safe only holds my mother's jewelry, the most important pieces. Assuming the villain hasn't taken those yet. With luck, your Mr. Barrow will supply us with his name. He's obviously a disgusting pig who's been blackmailing our parents and attempting to destroy our family."

It didn't take Belle and Honey long to read through the correspondence and documents, none of which proved particularly noteworthy. Finn replaced the marriage certificate and newspaper clipping in the hidden drawer and then put the other documents and letters back in place. However, he took the ledgers upstairs with him.

"Remember, keep your father away from his study tomorrow. We'll discuss our findings with him after the garden party."

"And make him tell us what else he's been hiding from us all these months." Belle sighed. "I wish we could cancel the party."

Honey agreed. "We'll have to politely reject Lord Wycke's invitation to his country home. I'm sure the scandal will have broken by then, and he won't want us around for his weekend party. I'll convey our apologies."

"I'm so sorry, Honey." The pain in Belle's voice was noticeable.

Finn ached for both of these innocents, for they had no hand in this disaster, but they would be the ones to suffer most for it. He could protect Belle and would do whatever he could to protect her sister, but he feared it wouldn't be enough. If news broke of their circumstances, who would be strong enough to not care and court Honey?

The three of them quietly made their way upstairs. Finn intended to disappear into Joshua's room with the ledgers, for he had a full night of reading ahead of him. First, he waited for Belle and Honey to enter their bedchambers.

Belle stayed by his side instead, kissing him on the lips. "Wake us if your brother is having difficulty or if you find anything of note in the ledgers. I think I'll sleep with Honey tonight. Otherwise, you'll both stay up all night, worried that I'll have another attack once I'm alone in my bed. I can't have each of you creeping in and out of my room all night long."

He cast her a mirthless smile. "Indeed, can't have us disturb your sleep."

She kissed him again. "I don't think I'd mind too much if I opened my eyes to find you looking at me."

Finn kissed her back and grinned. "Nor would I ever mind waking to your beautiful smile. Goodnight, love."

Once certain Belle and her sister were safely inside, he entered Joshua's room. His brother was stretched out on his bed with a hand over his eyes. He'd taken off his clothes, all but his trousers. "When you step into trouble, Finn, you really step in it. This is bad for them," he said, referring to Belle and Honey. "They'll be outcasts in Society."

"We'll support them, and so will the Farthingales. It'll all work out." He settled in a large chair by the hearth, lit a lamp for himself, and opened the ledgers, starting at a point six months ago and working his way forward. That seemed about the time this downward spiral began.

Joshua remained awake. "I'd help with the ledgers, but my head is pounding."

"I know, Josh. I have it in hand. It won't take me long to pick up on what's really been going on in the business."

"Finn, did you mean it when you told Belle that whatever happens, you still want to marry her?"

He glanced up from the ledgers. "Yes. Why? Do you have a problem with it?"

"No, of course not. I'm happy for you." He sank back against his pillows. "I just wondered how it felt to love someone so deeply, nothing else mattered but to protect them and make a good life for them. Is it a very odd feeling?"

Finn gave the question serious thought. "Surprisingly, no. It is a very right feeling. You'll know it when it hits you."

"Is it like being hit over the head with a candlestick? Lord, that thing was heavy. And how does someone the little size of Holly pack such a solid punch? I feel sorry for the man who tries to kiss her before she's ready. She's awfully young to be a widow. I wonder if she loved her husband."

"She's a Farthingale. I expect she did." He glanced down at the ledgers once more.

"But she had to have been very young when she married. Perhaps too young to understand what true and lasting love is all about."

Finn sighed. "Perhaps."

"Damn, she hit me so hard, I'm still seeing stars. So, this is what love feels like? I'm not sure I'm ready for it."

"Then why are you still going on about it?"

CHAPTER TWELVE

BELLE'S STOMACH WAS in knots, and she hardly slept, for how could she or her sister rest after what they'd learned? By morning, they were both distressed and exhausted. "Honey, there's nothing we can do about this horrible revelation. So, put it out of your mind. We'll deal with it tomorrow."

Honey nodded. "Agreed."

Belle peered out the window, somehow believing the world had been swallowed up. But in fact, the sun was shining, and there was a delightful breeze blowing into her sister's bedchamber. She hurried back to her own quarters, washing and dressing in preparation for the party that was to be held today.

While Honey stayed close to their mother to assist her in the morning chores, Belle found one excuse or another to hover in the hall, her purpose to prevent her father from entering his study and discovering his drawers had been broken into. Fortunately, her parents were in a particular dither preparing for the garden party, and since his foot was still paining him, he mostly sat in the drawing room and allowed the staff to attend him.

Holly, Dahlia, and Heather helped distract her parents as well, although only Holly knew the terrible secret revealed last night. Their mother spent most of her time between the kitchen and the elaborate tables set up outdoors in their garden, often accompanied by Honey or one of their cousins.

Belle had only to remain near the study and intercept anyone who approached it.

Her tension eased as guests began to arrive, mostly old friends of her parents who needed to be settled in their guest quarters because they would stay the night. For a few, it was too far to travel home after the party. Once again, her cousins stepped up to assist them, leaving Honey and Belle free to do whatever they needed to do.

Finn and Joshua had gone out earlier to meet their Bow Street runners. It hadn't taken them long to return. Belle was jumping out of her skin to know what they'd found out. Honey hurried over to join them the moment she spotted the two men striding toward Belle. "What news?"

Finn glanced around, surveying the guests now milling in and out of the drawing room and those casually sauntering through the house. "Not here. I don't want us to be overheard."

"Take a walk with us in the garden," Belle suggested. "Joshua, how are you feeling?"

"Wretched," he admitted. "Finn can tell you what we've learned. I need to sit in the shade with a tall drink. I'm fine, just feeling that lump on my brow."

Belle nodded sympathetically. "Holly feels terrible about it."

Joshua winced. "Not her fault. I should have kept my eye on the door."

After making certain Joshua was comfortably settled, she, Finn, and Honey walked outdoors. Finn led them beyond the garden, along a shaded walk. "Mr. Barrow and his colleague are waiting for us just around the corner. They'll stay in hiding, but I want you to know they're here and watching over both of you."

He continued to lead them down the shaded walk toward a thicket of hedgerows, a sister on each arm. To anyone else, their walk would appear quite innocent, most believing he was showing a romantic interest in Honey, because it was maddeningly obvious that even their family friends considered her damaged goods.

Belle tried not to let it anger her, but she couldn't help it. All her life, she'd accepted this attitude and had grown to believe it herself. If not for Finn, she would have spent her life believing she was inferior. He saw at once the insidious harm it had caused her in the subtle smiles they cast Honey and the pitying glances tossed her way.

He had no qualms declaring himself in love with her, but she was her own worst enemy. He was being quite patient with her and would never push her into a betrothal or marriage before she was ready. He'd said he would wait forever, but she knew it was not so. In any event, she knew her mind and would no longer hide her feelings for him. She loved him, and he deserved to know. He deserved to hear her say it.

Finn's mind was on her family's blackmailer, so Belle turned her attention to dealing with that matter.

"They've given us a name for your villain," Finn said. "A Lord Alliston Fortesque. Do either of you know him?"

Honey gasped and turned to Belle. "His son, Lawrence, was court- ing you shortly before we were sent down to London."

Belle rolled her eyes. "He wasn't really, but this explains his sud- den interest in me. Finn, it was fake. I could tell. His every word and action reeked of insincerity. But this explains why he bothered to call on me. His father probably pushed him to do it, hoping he could wheedle the formulas out of me. He wanted me for my nose. Why else would—"

"Why else would anyone want you? Damn it, Belle. Don't you dare belittle yourself."

She laughed and cast him a sweet, heartwarming smile. "My knight in shining armor. Will you challenge me to a duel if I continue to insult the woman you love?"

Finn shook his head and sighed. "I'm sorry, Belle. It tears me up inside to hear you say such things."

She gave his hand a light squeeze. "I know, and I will overcome it in time. But I've heard it for so long that's it's become a part of me."

"Fortesque's son was a fool if he didn't recognize the obvious beauty in you."

"Perhaps in time, he might have realized it, but I think the son was tossed into this mess just as we were. His father is the brains behind this nasty operation." She pursed her lips in thought. "Lawrence did not strike me as being very clever. Not nearly as clever as you. Or handsome as you. Or—"

Finn growled low in his throat, but it was a playful growl. "Stop, or I'll go down on my knee and propose to you again. Ah, here's Homer Barrow and his associate, Mick. Let me introduce them to you."

Homer Barrow reminded Belle of a kindly grandfather, the sort who would cheerfully take a horde of grandchildren on his lap and let them clamber all over his portly body. But his eyes were sharp and assessing, and he appeared to be quick-witted as well, the sort who could talk his way out of any dangerous scrape.

His face was jowly, and he had a prominent, bulbous nose. His companion, Mick, was a brawny man with a leathery face like that of a sailor used to spending long hours in the sun.

Belle smiled at them. "It is a pleasure to meet you, gentlemen."

They responded with equal politeness, although their accents were coarse. They quickly told her of what they'd learned about Lord Fortesque. "He may be of the Upper Crust, but his dealings are low," Homer said. "He's into some very shady business. Smuggling, gaming hells, pleasure dens, blackmail."

Mick nodded. "Especially blackmail. He sets up his marks, gets them drunk. Gets them talking. Gets them losing heavily at the gaming tables to the point of ruination, then he gives them a simple way out, or so they think."

"Tell me a secret, and I'll eliminate your debt, is what he tells them." Homer shook his head and sighed. "Once he learns the secret, he tears up their marker. But he doesn't really let them off, because once they sober up, they realize what they've done and are willing to pay him a king's ransom to keep it quiet. That's when he really begins to squeeze them. Now, he doesn't merely have his original target, but everyone else involved in the secret."

The two runners looked to Finn for guidance.

He nodded. "The ladies know. We searched their father's desk and discovered his secret."

Belle frowned. "But I don't understand. My father doesn't drink heavily or gamble. He would never frequent the sort of establishments run by this wicked man."

Finn's expression darkened. "But your uncle would. And did."

Honey gasped. "Uncle Jacob betrayed his own sister? How could he? After all she and Father have done for him! Why couldn't he destroy himself, give up one of his own secrets?"

Belle knew the answer. "He had none of significance. So, he gave away..." She turned away, unable to finish the thought. "How do we fix this, Finn? We can't make Fortesque forget what he knows. Besides, he's probably told his son as well. Perhaps Runyon, too."

Finn set a hand on her shoulder to comfort her. "Runyon's just an enforcer. He isn't told anything other than to go around town and collect Fortesque's ill-gotten gains."

"I wish they'd all get struck by lightning or fall off a cliff or drown," Honey muttered, then realized she'd spoken the thought aloud. "I didn't mean for us to actually do away with all of them, much as they deserve punishment."

Finn cast her a mirthless smile. "I know. But I have a plan."

Belle looked up at him in alarm. "It doesn't involve you going to his establishment, does it? He'll kill you if he suspects you intend to bring down his operation."

His hand remained on her shoulder, lightly caressing her with the swirl of his thumbs. "I'm going to bring it down and bury him in debris up to his eyeballs."

"Finn! You can't! He has men protecting him. They'll stop you before you can touch him."

He shrugged. "Who says I ever have to lay a hand on him?"

Belle did not like the way Finn spoke so calmly. His Bow Street runners were similarly calm. No, they were icy. All three of them. Cold, hard. Determined and possibly lethal. What were they planning? "Finn…" She coughed. "You…can't…" She coughed again, her panic rising as she realized she was about to have an attack.

Her next breath came out in a wheeze.

Honey gasped. "Oh, Belle! Not now. Keep her calm, Finn. I'll get something for her."

As Honey ran off, she suddenly felt Finn lift her in his arms and carry her a short distance from the runners, who were looking on in dismay. He carried her to a large, fallen oak that had yet to be cut for kindling, settling on its trunk and cradling her on his lap. "Belle, calm yourself," he said in a deep, resonant tone that warmed her very insides. "There'll be no weapons fired. No confrontation of that sort."

"What if…he…" Her lungs were squeezing the breath out of her.

"What if he ignores the rules of engagement and shoots me? He won't. I'll meet him in a ladies' tea shop or in the vaunted halls of one of the colleges, if I must meet him at all. The only battle we will have will be a battle of words. I've already been shot once. I'd be dead if not for your cousin, Violet, saving me. So, I have no desire to test my luck again."

"I want…" She coughed.

"You want to believe me?"

She nodded, surprised by how well he could read her thoughts. But this is how strongly they were connected to each other. Finn had known at once. She had known it, too, felt it the first time they'd ever met. Felt it the moment his lips had touched hers to breathe life back in her and his hands had pressed on her chest to keep her heart pumping.

She had been struggling to deny it ever since. "I…"

"Hush, love. These runners are the best in all of England. I didn't send them into the bowels merely looking for the culprit behind the blackmail scheme. I also sent them in to discover the culprit's weakness. Everybody has a vulnerable spot."

She circled her arms around his neck and rested her head against his shoulder. At the same time, she closed her eyes and willed herself to regain the rhythm of her breathing. It helped that she was in Finn's arms. She felt the caress of his fingers against her cheek, the warmth of his lips as he kissed her brow. She felt the strength in his big, muscled body and tried to draw from it.

Her breaths were almost back to normal by the time Honey returned with a ginger tea. She drank it down and allowed its healing properties to work its way through her chest. Finn was watching her intently. He had one eyebrow arched, as though lovingly warning her not to pass a comment about her weakness, or he would challenge her to a duel to defend her honor.

Once she felt herself well enough to stand on her own, she rose from his lap with great reluctance. "We had better return to the party. I don't want my parents to worry." She then turned to the two Bow Street runners. "Thank you for all you are doing for my family."

Homer nodded. "Happy to be of service. Are ye feeling better now, Miss Farthingale?"

She smiled at him. "I've just spent the last ten minutes in the arms of the handsomest man in England. How can I not feel just perfect?"

She, Finn, and Honey walked back to the house to mingle with their guests. Belle wasn't sure what she would do if Fortesque dared show his face, but to her relief, he was not in attendance at their party. No doubt, he found it too dangerous to socially engage with those he was bleeding dry.

The party passed uneventfully after that, the day remaining warm and sunny, with little more than a light breeze wafting in the air. The table linens gently billowed in the breeze, and the wind rustled through the leaves.

Belle was sensitive to the fragrant scents stirred in the air…roses warming in the sun, a lingering dew on the grass, the sweet, honeyed scent of the hedgerows surrounding their grounds. Of course, each food course, as it was set out, also captured her attention. The earthy scent of fish and game hen, the aromatic scent of ripe fruit, and the array of pungent cheeses. But the scent she loved best was the freshly baked bread, hot and crusty, still steaming as it was carried straight from the kiln onto the tables to cool.

The tables were bowed and groaning by the time the desserts were laid out. Their savory allure beckoned even those who vowed they'd eaten too much and could not manage a bite more. Yet somehow, everyone found room for buttered apple tarts, the delicate and ornate tennis cake which served as a centerpiece for the dessert table, Banbury cakes, blancmange, lemon cream, and syllabub.

Belle set aside her distress and managed to enjoy conversing with old friends again. She introduced them to Finn, since he remained by her side. It quickly became clear to everyone they were a courting couple. Having him beside her felt quite splendid. He wasn't overly doting, for it was not in his manner to be a fawning toady.

However, it was in his nature to be protective. She knew he was struggling with it, but he didn't stifle her as they moved through the crowd and stopped to engage in conversation with those she had not seen in a while. She no longer cared that everyone first glanced across the garden to where Honey stood, as though expecting her to shove through the crowd and claim it was all a mistake, that Finn was really courting her.

But after those first few glances of confusion, there came acceptance and genuinely good wishes for her and Finn.

After the party, Belle finally had a moment to relax. Most of their friends had returned to their homes. A few remained here for the night but had already retired to their guest chambers and would leave first thing in the morning. Her family and Joshua had retired to their rooms, leaving her and Finn alone downstairs to close up the house and douse the lamps and sconces. "It was a nice party, Belle."

"If not for the anvil dangling over our heads." She cast him a wry smile. "I'd hoped to talk to my parents this evening, but we may as well wait until the last of our guests leave us tomorrow morning. I don't want to put off the discussion any longer. I can see this secret has devastated them. Perhaps it will be worse for them once they realize we know, but I hope not. I think they will be relieved...or at least accepting of it, once we tell them."

He nodded. "You must be tired. Let me walk you up to your bed-chamber."

When they got to her door, she didn't want him to leave. Of course, she couldn't invite him in. Yet, she couldn't bear to be apart from him.

He must have sensed her yearning. He tipped his head toward her room. "Is your maid in there?"

"No, I dismissed her earlier."

He glanced at her gown. "Need help untying your laces?"

"I was going to ask Honey...but...would you mind handling the task?"

"Mother in heaven," he murmured, turning her slightly and nudging her arm up so he could see the lacing along her side. There was no way to loosen the intricate ties without his hand grazing the fullness of her breast. "Ah, Belle. Perhaps this isn't such a good idea. You ought to wake Honey."

"No, I'd like you to do it." She was horrified by what she'd just said but was not going to take it back. Instead of apologizing, she opened her door and drew him inside.

He was frowning, not the response she'd hoped for, but understood this was his protective nature acting up again, even to protect her against himself. "Belle, are you certain?"

She nodded and shut the door behind them. "I don't know what will happen tomorrow, and at this moment, I don't care. I know my parents will not respond well when they find out we know their secret. I expect the entire household will be in an uproar. The servants will know something is going on, and some might even figure it out."

"Servants know how to be discreet."

"I hope so. Some of them are truly loyal and will take it to their graves. Others, I don't know. But the greater danger is Lord Fortesque. Despite your plan, there's no guarantee my family will be saved from ruin."

"There is never any certainty in life." He stood in the center of her room, his arms folded across his chest so that he would not reach out and take her into his embrace. He was still wary of what she was doing. No doubt, he understood why she'd invited him in and asked for his assistance in removing her gown.

However, she was not having much success in tempting him.

She sighed in frustration.

The Book of Love said all men had two brains, the low and the high. She was trying to appeal to Finn's low brain. The book ought to have warned that seduction was not as simple as it appeared, despite a man's low brain propensities.

"I suppose you're wondering why I've brought you in here." She tried to sound casual.

She heard the affectionate humor in his tone as he replied. "To lure me down the path of wickedness and defile me, I expect." Then his manner turned serious. "Perhaps it is the other way around. I am not averse to having my way with you, but it must be for the right reasons."

She finally mustered the courage to meet his gaze, and her heart melted. Truly, this man was stunning. But she also saw the intelligence and compassion in his exquisite eyes. "What do you love about me,

Finn?"

He unfolded his arms and stepped toward her but did not touch her. "Everything. I love that your name is Bluebell. I love your smile and the impudent arch of your eyebrows. I love your sharp mind, and don't roll your eyes at me. I could not bear ten minutes in your company if you were a simple-minded peahen. Of course, I love your body. Don't ask me why. I think it's just my low brain response. The shape and symmetry of you...meaning your beautiful breasts."

She took no offense and laughed softly.

"That, too. Your sweet, soft laugh. I love the sparkle in your eyes when you look at me. You stir all of my senses. Now that I've read that book, I understand just what happens when one falls in love."

"You haven't mentioned my affliction yet. Is there not an element of pity that draws you to me?"

He took her question with surprising seriousness. "I won't deny there is a little of that, but it is only one very small part of the entirety of reasons. In order for us to gain commitment and intimacy, we have to connect with each other on many levels. I think of it as interlocking parts. Our parts fit. You have a vulnerability, and I have a protective nature that needs to rescue you. I'm a smart man, and my mind often speeds ahead, leaving others behind. You have no trouble keeping up with me. You are secure in your own talents and can run circles around me when it comes to those ciphers."

"It's just a game."

"Men make careers and gain respected reputations on such games." He arched an eyebrow and grinned. "Here's one for you. What is broken merely by your speaking its name?"

"Here I am trying to seduce you, and you wish to play word games?"

"Oh, I'll get to the seduction shortly. But it's important for you to understand why I'm in love with you. You're worried I'll come to my senses and distance myself from you and your disgraced family."

She nodded.

"It will never happen. Have you figured out the riddle yet?"

She nodded again. "It's simple. What is broken merely by my speaking its name? The answer is silence. If I speak the word, then I've broken the silence."

He laughed. "I knew you'd get it. This is why I love you, Belle. Your face is beautiful. Your body is beautiful. Your mind is sharp. Your heart is gentle and compassionate. How have I chosen badly?"

He finally reached for her and took her in his arms. "If you want me in here...if you've thought it through and are willing to accept the consequences..."

She nodded. "I have."

"By consequences, I mean marrying me. Whether or not we're caught. I want you, Belle. I want you with an ache that burns in my soul. I'm giving you fair warning, if you let me slip the gown off your luscious body, I'm taking that as your consent to marry me."

She rested her head against his chest and nodded. "I will marry you. But I also want you to know that you may change your mind until the moment we exchange our vows. After that, I will hold you to every promise made to me in the eyes of the Church and our holy union."

"Agreed." He tipped her chin up and kissed her lightly on the lips. It was a long but gentle kiss. After a moment, he drew back and began to unpin her hair, running his fingers through it as it slowly tumbled down her back and over her shoulders.

He smiled.

The smile reached into his eyes, reflecting his enjoyment.

He lowered his head and kissed her again, this time untying her laces with a deftness that revealed he'd done this before. She knew by the gentle urgency in his next kiss, and the struggle to restrain himself, that she meant something important to him.

He slipped the gown off her body and slowly, sensually removed her undergarments until she stood barefoot, her toes curling into the elegant, Belgian weave carpet. She wore only her chemise, although she may as well have been wearing nothing at all since his gaze seemed to burn straight through the sheer fabric to rake over her bare skin.

He had yet to do more than kiss her...and undress her, of course. She did not realize how exciting it could be to have him remove her clothes. Every part of her body was throbbing, and she felt an urgent thrum in the most unexpected places.

Instead of removing her chemise, he stopped and began to undress himself, taking off his jacket, vest, and cravat. He chuckled as she took each garment from him and neatly folded it over her chair. "Next time," he said, "we'll be tossing our clothes haphazardly on the floor, sparing not a care for them."

"We will?"

He nodded.

Her breath caught as he removed his shirt to reveal the strength and breadth of his body. His stomach was lean and flat, exposing taut, rippled flesh. His chest was hard and smooth to the touch. His arms were as hard as the trunk of an oak tree and felt quite warm as she ran her palms along their bulging muscles. She felt the ugly, puckered scar where he'd been shot. But it only added to his allure. Nor could she resist curling her fingers in the spray of dark hair across his chest.

Unable to help herself, she closed her eyes, eager to soak in every sensation. *Touch.* She ran her hands along his arms and felt every sculpted sinew. She reached up and feathered kisses along his neck and jaw and finally upon his lips. He tasted of wine and currants from the Banbury cakes he'd eaten earlier. *Taste.*

He growled low in his throat, seemingly pleased she was not behaving like a shy miss. She loved the sensual *sound* of his satisfaction. But how far did she dare go? Would he be horrified and disgusted if she became exceedingly wanton? How far was too far for a young lady when encouraging a man to claim her body?

She knew she ought to be having second thoughts. But being with Finn felt so very right. Her mind was in too much of a muddle to make sense of all the reasons why, but did it really matter? He was perfect for her, and he'd told her she was perfect for him.

He was very good at analyzing things.

She trusted him, and he always made perfect sense.

Yes, that word—perfect—always popped into her head when thinking of Finn.

She liked the way he looked at her, as though he wanted to devour her.

He always smelled divine, too. Today, his scent was of musk and male heat. She recognized another of her cologne fragrances called Gladiator.

Oh, it suited this man!

The fragrance was a hint of spice mingled with essence of musk deer. The scent of musk alone tended to entice women, but adding that trace of spice seemed to turn up the furnace, somehow arousing a woman's senses to the point of wanting to claw the shirt off a man's back.

Indeed, it was potent.

She knew what was in the formula. Indeed, she had created it. And yet, she was helpless to resist it.

If this was not the scent of love, she did not know what else could be.

"Belle," he said with a soft, laughing groan. "Why are you sniffing me?"

"Oh, forgive me. I was going through the senses in my mind, and you know how important the sense of smell is to me. You're wearing Gladiator."

"Yes, I didn't realize it was another of yours. I'm not surprised."

"It suits you."

He ran his hands up her body to ease the chemise off her and toss it onto his pile of clothing. He drew in a long, deep breath as he studied her, absorbing and memorizing her every curve. "You're beautiful."

He cupped her face in his hands and gently tilted her head upward, at the same time lowering his mouth to hers. The first kiss was sweet. The second, deeper and longer. The third was not a kiss so much as a trail of kisses from her cheek, to her jaw, a few nibbles at her ear and along her neck. Then he cupped her breast and bent his head to suckle the rosy bud.

If she were a bird capable of flying, she'd be soaring off the floor this very instant. "Finn!" Fireworks exploded in her body. "Merciful heaven, what are you doing?"

"Touching you, love. Tasting you." He started to ease away. "Do you want me to stop?"

"Are you mad? Of course not. It's just...oh. Do you know what you are doing to me?"

"I have an inkling." He lifted her in his arms. "There's more. I've hardly gotten started."

"You're only just starting?"

He sighed. "I had better stop. We aren't married and—"

"We will be, Finn. Unless you change your mind. If you do, then this is even more important to me, for I won't have any other man touch me. How could I when he isn't you? My reluctance was never about my feelings for you."

"I know, love." He carried her to bed, setting her down on her back while he settled over her, his elbows bent to absorb the brunt of his weight atop her.

Then there were no more words, no more gazing into his exquisite eyes as she closed her own and simply took in each sensation. She never understood the power of the senses until this moment. Before, they'd been just words on a page in a book about love. But as he suckled and teased the peak of one breast and then shifted to suckle the other, his hands roamed along her body, setting little fires wherever he touched. She knew their hearts would be bound forever after this night.

"Lord, your scent is intoxicating."

She didn't understand what he meant by it. "I'm not wearing perfume or fragrant oils. Is it the oatmeal soap again? And I did use a little bit of lavender to wash my hair for the party."

"It's the natural scent of you. The womanly scent of your skin. Your essence stripped bare." He kissed the swell of her breast and began to kiss his way further down her body.

He suddenly stopped himself and groaned.

"Don't, Finn. I'm not afraid of anything with you. Why did you stop?"

"You're a virgin."

She wasn't certain why this was suddenly important. "Are you afraid to hurt me?"

"No, this ought to be quite pleasurable for you. But it will shock you."

"More pleasurable than shocking? Or more shocking than pleasurable?"

He kissed her lightly on the belly. "More pleasurable by far...once you get over the initial surprise."

"Show me." When she smiled, he spread her legs and eased his shoulders between them. She didn't stop him. She was already wild for him, and he'd already touched her intimately *there* with his fingers as though to ready her for something exquisite.

When his mouth closed over her slick core, she thought she would expire. Whatever sensations of pleasure she'd experienced moments before were nothing to the molten heat she now experienced at the touch of his lips and tongue. Dear heaven! Is this what their nights would be as husband and wife?

She wanted this.

She wanted him to know her in every way, to inhale her scent and touch her, taste her. Kiss her. She wanted to know him in the same way. She wanted to claim him, and at the same time, belong to him.

As he continued to work his wicked magic, she felt herself burning up inside.

Not merely burning, but a strange pressure was building within her body. She didn't know quite how to describe it, perhaps like the hot bubble of a volcano about to erupt. The pressure built and overwhelmed her and finally took over her body, sending it soaring to the sky in a great, fiery burst. "Finn!"

He continued his relentless onslaught even as she gasped and softly cried his name over and over again. "Finn. Finn."

The fire would not stop. Waves of heat flowed through her body, rolling like an unstoppable current through every limb and pore. She tingled and shuddered several times before her body exploded in an exquisite burst of pleasure.

She'd heard whispers from her married cousins about the joys of sharing intimacy with the one they loved. They'd spoken of stars and fireworks, and she finally understood why. With Finn, she saw starlight and moonbeams and comets streaking across the sky.

Finn rolled off her as she began to calm, taking her in his arms and holding her gently. "I love you, Belle. I love you with all my heart," he said over and over again until she was once more herself.

No, she would never be herself again, for a part of her belonged to him now.

She snuggled against him, her face burrowing into his chest and her arms wrapping around his neck. He was unclothed from the waist up. She was completely unclothed. Yet, she was glad she was. She wanted to feel him against her skin. His body was hot, perhaps not on fire as hers had been, but he was clearly affected by what they'd just done.

Well, he'd been the one actively doing. She'd been actively receiving. "Finn, there should be more. Shouldn't there be?"

She felt his hardness against her hip.

"Yes, love. But not tonight. I'll have my turn next time. Were I to claim you now, it would leave a mark on your sheets."

She nodded against his chest, knowing it was for the best. If he took her innocence, he would never back out of marrying her. Not that what they'd done only moments ago was remotely innocent. She'd never realized how wonderfully naughty such pleasures could be. Indeed, she never knew such pleasures existed until Finn had shown her.

But despite her wanton behavior, she was still...a maiden.

It sounded awful.

He'd left her in her virginal state on purpose, not for his sake, but for hers. He meant to protect her innocence if things went wrong when dealing with Lord Fortesque.

She closed her eyes and held onto him tightly. "I love you, Finn."

He laughed affectionately. "Bravo, sweetheart. I never thought to hear you say it so soon."

"I never thought I would, but it's important for you to know how I feel. And how much I fear your confronting Lord Fortesque. I've just found you. I don't want to lose you."

"You won't, love."

"Promise me; and mean it, Finn."

"I promise. I have no intention of allowing that fiend to get the better of me."

If only she could believe him. If only his promise was enough to keep him safe. But Belle was so worried. What would happen when Finn confronted Lord Fortesque, that horrid beast of Oxford?

CHAPTER THIRTEEN

D AWN BROKE TO reveal another beautiful June morning in the offing. Finn sat quietly at the breakfast table with Belle, her family, and the guests who had remained overnight. They would depart shortly, and then the difficult business would start.

Finn couldn't take his eyes off Belle throughout the morning. What they'd done last night! Glory to the heavens! He'd never imagined having such a night before they were officially wed. He'd never imagined doing more than kissing her gently and then leaving her bedchamber before anything more happened.

He ought to have known he had the resistance of a jellyfish when it came to this girl. Yes, he was a low, spineless jellyfish, for it had taken nothing to turn his thoughts to mindless rutting. One glance at her spectacular body, and he was lost to all reason.

Nor could he stop himself from smiling at her now. Every time he did, her cheeks turned fiery red. It was a good feeling, knowing she'd enjoyed her first adventure. That she'd trusted him, had chosen him to be the only man to ever touch her. It made him preen like a peacock.

He tried not to smile again, but he couldn't help it.

She shot daggers at him with her gaze, blushed again, then shook her head and joined him in the intimate smile.

Yes, his heart was lost to this girl.

By the time the Farthingales finally saw the last of their guests off, it was late morning. Finn turned to Belle. "Care to take a walk with me?"

Belle's cousin, Dahlia, looked at her. "Holly is taking Heather and me into Oxford for the day. Joshua said he would accompany us. Would you like to join us?"

"No," Belle replied. "Honey and I had better stay behind to help Mother. I'm sure there's lots to be done putting the house back to order."

Dahlia frowned. "Oh, how thoughtless of us. We'll stay and help out."

"Nonsense," Honey said, taking Dahlia by the arm and walking her toward the door where Joshua and Holly were already standing. "We'll be done well before supper. I'll tell you what, if we finish early, we'll join you at the tea shop at three o'clock."

"But don't wait for us," Belle added, herding Heather out as well. She lowered her voice to a whisper. "Father's leg is still sore, and Mother looks a little fatigued. We might just stay home and look after them today. I'll pretend it's me who's feeling under the weather. I don't wish to embarrass them. Father, especially. He's awfully proud."

Her cousins nodded conspiratorially and grinned at Finn, who had followed them into the entry hall. "We understand." They peered over Belle's head to stare at him. "Will you ask for her hand today? Is this why you really want us out from underfoot?"

"Yes," Finn replied.

Belle gasped. "He's jesting."

Dahlia rolled her eyes. "Honestly, Belle. We all can see it. He's madly in love with you. He practically devoured you for breakfast." They hurried off, giggling.

Belle waved cheerily to her cousins while their carriage rolled down the drive on its way into the heart of Oxford. Once they were out of sight, she turned to him in dismay. "Oh, I'm dreading this."

Finn took her hand as they entered the house. "I know, love. I'll be by your side. Ready?"

She nodded.

Finn kept her hand in his, telling himself it was to quietly support her. But he also knew what had happened between them last night was something quite extraordinary, and he simply did not want to let her go.

He knew Belle had a beautiful body, but to see her in the moonlight, her tawny curls in a lush cascade down her back, her skin as soft as silk and her eyes glowing as bright as starlight, he felt as though he'd stepped into a dream that he never wanted to end.

He quickly shook out of the thought when they returned to the drawing room. Neither sister was smiling as they dismissed the footmen before shutting the door behind them and drawing up chairs beside their parents. For Belle and her sister, this was no dream but the start of a nightmare.

"What's wrong, my dears?" their father asked, his love for his girls so obvious, it tugged at Finn's heart.

This is how he would feel if he and Belle had daughters. His heart would be so full of love for them, it would be filled to bursting. Was it any wonder the man was eating his guts out over this sad affair?

Belle took a deep breath. "We know."

Her parents exchanged panicked glances before her father spoke again. "What are you talking about?"

"We know Lord Fortesque has been blackmailing you. And we know why." She turned to her mother and gave her hand a light squeeze as tears began to fill her mother's eyes. "We found the hidden drawer and the proof of your first marriage."

Both parents glanced at Finn in alarm.

He was the outsider, and they feared he would reveal their secret.

Belle looked up at him with love in her eyes. "We can speak freely with Finn. He knows everything. He's reviewed your ledgers, and he's the one who found the secret drawer."

Finn stepped forward to stand by Belle's side. "What happened in

153

your past is safe with me. I intend to marry Belle. Nothing will ever change how I feel about her."

"You're serious about marrying our Belle?" Her father sounded so beaten, and yet so desperately hopeful, it hurt to look at him.

Finn nodded.

"Thank goodness," her mother said in a quiet sob.

"Mother," Honey said gently, "tell us what happened."

Their parents' faces were ashen, both of them openly sobbing. "I married young. He went off to sea shortly after we were wed, and then I was told he'd died. I met your father soon after. We built a wonderful, happy life."

Her husband put his arm around her shoulders. "Never fear, my love. We'll get through this together...as we've gotten through all of our difficulties. I think Mr. Brayden has put the sentiment quite well. Nothing will ever change how I feel about you."

Belle's mother shook her head. "I've brought this shame upon us. I've destroyed my own daughters."

Belle and Honey took turns hugging her. "You haven't. You've given us nothing but love and made a good home for us."

"But it's all gone to ashes," their mother said, her voice a broken whisper. "Lord Fortesque will never relent. He'll drain us of everything and leave us as beggars in the street."

"He won't. This will end." Belle turned to Finn with hopeful eyes. "This is why we asked Finn to join us. He's brilliant. He'll find a solution to this problem."

Belle's father studied him. "How? It isn't possible. The man is too powerful. He is well connected here in Oxford."

Finn folded his arms across his chest. "My family is just as powerful, if not more so. My cousin, Marcus Brayden, was invested with the title, Earl of Kinross, because of his military valor in service to the Crown. He is a favorite of the royal family. My brother is Earl of Westcliff, and another of my cousins is Earl of Exmoor. Marcus was a

THE SCENT OF LOVE

general in the army. His brother Caleb still holds that rank and remains in active service. My own younger brothers are military liaisons to Parliament. That's just the men in my family. I haven't mentioned my own connections outside the family, which are extensive. And if all else fails, there is always my mother, Lady Miranda Grayfell. You do not wish to cross paths with her when she is in ill temper."

"Young man, I'm sure your connections are quite impressive. But you are dealing with a dangerous man. If you confront him, he will kill you."

Belle gasped.

Finn put a hand on her shoulder to calm her. He knew her father's words had frightened her, and he wanted to strangle the man just now. Did he not realize that fear would trigger one of Belle's attacks? Her breaths were coming faster. She began to cough. "It won't happen, love. This is what Fortesque wants you all to believe, but he's vulnerable."

"Finn…" She coughed again.

"Belle, listen to me. It is only a matter of time before someone strikes back, and he knows it will happen. I will be the one to strike him hard. I won't be alone. I'll have experienced men with me, and I'll take precautions."

She placed a hand over her heart. "How can you be sure?"

"You are brilliant at ciphers, but my talent is in understanding people, even the lowest scoundrels. His son is his weak spot. All he's done, everything he's built up over the years has been for his boy. He's sent him to the best schools, given him an elegant upbringing, and introduced him to the best families."

Her father frowned. "The boy even courted Belle for a time."

"He wasn't courting me, Father. We all know Lord Fortesque would have ordered Lawrence to break off the supposed courtship the moment he got his hands on my formulas." She rolled her eyes. "As if

I'd ever be so foolish as to give them over to him."

Her mother dabbed at her tears and sniffled. "I thought young Fortesque sincerely cared for you."

"He didn't," Belle said.

Gad, her parents were naive. Finn was glad she and Honey had better sense. Still, he did not wish to hurt their feelings. "Perhaps he did like Belle. But it is irrelevant since Fortesque would not have given his consent to their marriage. He intends his son to marry into the aristocracy."

"And he'll succeed," her father muttered. "We'll be ruined, and his son will be married to the daughter of a duke."

Finn held on to his patience, for they sounded so defeated. He could not bear to hear the utter resignation in their voices. "It will never happen if his son is disgraced and imprisoned."

Belle looked up at him, startled. "How? His father is a lord. Young Fortesque would never be sent to prison."

"He would for treason. He'd be hanged if it could be proved."

Belle was getting agitated again. "Are you speaking of planting false evidence? Finn, you cannot do this. Two wrongs don't make a right."

He took her gently by the shoulders and turned her to face him. "Whether I do so or not is completely up to Lord Fortesque. Do you believe for one moment he is not up to his ears in dirty dealings? Selling weapons to the French in wartime? Trading military secrets? Perhaps it was small amounts, not intended to have a serious impact. But such is the nature of this man. Nothing is sacred to him."

"But his son must be innocent of this."

"Of treason? Perhaps. I don't care. So are you innocent of all that is happening to you. Has he shown you any mercy?" He held onto her shoulders, still taking care to be gentle despite his rage toward that vermin. "Belle, how can his son not know what his father is doing? He was courting you to get your formulas. He may not have been happy about it. He may not approve of his father's dealings, but he is doing nothing to stop him."

"He is living an easy and carefree life off the misery of others," Honey added with disdain.

"You don't want me to use force," Finn said, "so let me use my wits. But know this, if Lord Fortesque will not see reason, then neither will I. Your safety and that of your sister is my only concern. If he hurts you, then I will hurt his son because this is the only thing that will destroy him. I will make it clear to him. He is not a stupid man. He will understand that he wins by losing this battle."

Her parents were gaping at him.

Belle was distraught, but her breaths were no longer erratic, and she was not coughing. "You mustn't go to him alone. He'll shoot you."

"No, love. He won't."

"How can you be certain?"

"Because if I am shot, his son will be shot. If I am spared, his son will be spared. Simple."

Her father seemed to hold the same concerns as Belle. "Don't underestimate this man, Mr. Brayden. I'm not sure he has a heart. You think he loves his son and is doing all of this to provide an easy life for the young man. But if pushed too far, there's no telling what he will do."

"I know. I understand the nature of a cornered beast."

Belle's father ran a trembling hand through his thinning, gray hair. "Girls, I know this is small consolation to you, but I want you to know that I've married your mother...remarried her quietly as soon as we learned Fenton had died. I wish this were enough to erase the cruel stain of your births. If I could fix your situation, I would. You'll inherit all I have, and all of the Farthingale family will support you if the truth of your..."

"Illegitimacy," Honey said, for their father could not speak the word.

"You are my sweethearts, the best daughters a man could ever have. I detest how the world will view you. It is unfair. I'll protect you the best I can. Belle, marry this man. You have my blessing. Cherish him. Love is a rare and wonderful thing. My heart is at ease knowing he will always take care of you and protect you. But my dear, beautiful Honey..." He couldn't look at her as he continued. "I shall pray fervently every day that you will find a man who has the decency to see beyond this tarnish."

"Don't worry, Father. I was never that keen on marrying, anyway. Even if our perfume shops are stolen from us, I'm sure Uncle John or Rose will allow me a role in their businesses. I'm good at what I do. Selling perfume is not so different from selling fabrics or Rose's beautiful glassworks and porcelain."

"Let me put my plan in motion," Finn said. "I won't confront him today. Perhaps not even tomorrow. It will take a few days to set it up properly."

"What shall we do in the meantime?" Belle asked.

He regarded her tenderly. "Prepare for a wedding."

CHAPTER FOURTEEN

BELLE FELT SO odd preparing for a wedding at the same time Finn was preparing to wage battle against an unmerciful foe. She tried to concentrate on this happy event, but couldn't. Dahlia and Heather were browsing wide-eyed through the modiste's shop while Honey and Holly remained in the dressing room with her. She was trying on gowns, merely samples available for anyone to try on. The modiste and her helpers were running in and out with more fabric samples suitable for a bridal trousseau.

"These are materials from the Farthingale millworks," the modiste said, skimming her hand lovingly over several bolts of luminescent satin that left all of them in awe.

"They look like faerie cloths. Woven with faerie magic," Holly said. "Look how they shimmer and change colors depending on the way they are held. Have you ever seen anything like them?"

Honey nodded. "They're quite beautiful."

"This one will make an exquisite ball gown for you." The modiste held up a bolt of emerald silk. "But let's set it aside for now. Your wedding gown is the most important. We must decide on that fabric first."

Belle nodded. "I prefer something simpler for my wedding."

"I have just the thing." The woman returned within moments carrying several more bolts of pastel silks. "Any of these will do. What do you think?"

Holly gasped. "I'd consider remarrying just for the chance to wear a wedding gown of any of these colors."

Belle chose silk of palest amber because it captured the amber flecks of her eyes and the reddish-gold of her hair. "I think Finn will like this one."

Everyone around her laughed. "I doubt he'll care," Honey said. "Men never notice this sort of thing. He'll only remember how he felt when he first saw you in it."

"And then he'll be waiting impatiently for the day to end so he can strip it off you," Holly teased. "But the fabric is truly beautiful."

Belle studied her cousin. Holly had been a widow several years now. She still wore drab, widow's colors. It seemed a shame. She wasn't much older than they were. No one would consider her on the shelf yet. "What about you, Holly? Surely you can do with a new gown or two."

She shook her head emphatically. "My sisters are to have their turn in Society. I'm quite happy to chaperone them. I am not putting myself on the marriage mart any time soon."

When they finished with the modiste, they went past their perfume shop and stopped in for a few moments. Mrs. Wynne and her staff happily greeted them. The shop was busy, as usual, and Mrs. Wynne assigned one of her assistants to attend to them. While her cousins tried on the latest perfumes, Belle went in back to inspect her laboratory, and Honey went into the office to check on the daily accounts.

Belle was relieved nothing had been touched since the last time they were in the shop. But when she peered out the back window, she saw Runyon standing there, staring back at her with an evil grin on his face.

She hastily drew away, placing her hand over her heart to steady its frantic beats.

She had sensed they were being watched even at the modiste shop.

Obviously, Runyon was following her.

What should she do?

Finn would tell her to do nothing. He would want her to run straight to him and tell him what she'd seen. Sighing, she knew this is what she had to do. Warn Finn. Report her concerns to him. Do not confront Runyon on her own. There was no other choice. She had no weapon, and Runyon was twice her size and a trained fighter.

She returned to the front of the shop and peered out the window to look for the Bow Street runners. She couldn't see them and wasn't certain she could count on them being close by. Perhaps they were assisting Finn now.

"Is something wrong?" Dahlia asked her.

"No, just thinking up a new scent. Are you thirsty? Shall we stop for tea?"

"A splendid idea," Heather said. "I could do with a strawberry tart...or two or three."

The cousins walked out, each with a bottle of perfume.

Belle and Honey bid Mrs. Wynne farewell but said nothing more for fear she might unwittingly give something of their plans away.

"Honey," Belle whispered when they were once more out on the street. "Runyon was standing behind the shop. I think he is following us. I sensed someone was watching us when we were at the modiste. You know, the creepy feeling that sends tingles shooting up your spine. If I see him at the tea shop, then it will confirm he's been assigned to follow us."

"Oh, Belle. Let's be careful. Make sure we all stay close. Thankfully, Abner will come around with our carriage. He won't let anyone get close enough to harm us, but I fear it is you they really want. You are the one who creates our scents."

"I'm going to tell Finn."

"Yes, you must. And what of the Bow Street runners Finn brought with him from London? Shouldn't they be following us as well? Have you seen them?"

Belle pursed her lips in worry. "No, I haven't seen them since yesterday. Perhaps Finn wanted them to go with him today."

"It makes sense." Honey nodded. "They're trained men. He'll need them to watch his back. And what of Joshua? I haven't seen him since early this morning. What do you think he's up to?"

"It's quite frustrating. Finn won't tell me anything about his plans. I'm not sure I like that. We're to be married soon. Shouldn't he confide in me?"

Honey locked her arm in Belle's as they walked to the tea shop. "He's a good man. He must have his reasons for keeping us in the dark."

"I hope he doesn't intend to maim Lord Fortesque. Seriously, Honey. I'll never forgive myself if I've turned him into a killer. He had such a fierce look on his face when we first confronted Mama and Papa."

"Do you remember Uncle John's favorite expression? He always says people don't change. If Finn has it in him to kill, then he's always had it in him."

Belle nodded. "But he's never had to use that ruthless trait before. What if he does have the killer instinct, and now I've brought it out in him with a vengeance? This is what worries me."

"There's nothing you can do about it, Belle. Stop worrying. And for pity's sake, don't try to handle any of this on your own. You'll get us all killed."

They caught up with their cousins and spent the rest of the afternoon chatting about the wedding over tea and cakes. Belle knew she had to confront Finn this evening. He simply had to tell her what he was planning. She had no intention of doing anything foolish, but she had to know what was going on. If plans went awry, she and Honey needed to protect themselves. Indeed, if plans went *badly* awry, they needed to form their own plan to rush in and save Finn.

To her surprise, Finn and Joshua did not return in time for supper.

Her parents retired early, leaving them to entertain their cousins. They read together. They played some silly party games. But as midnight approached, Dahlia and Heather could no longer keep their eyes open. Holly herded them upstairs, leaving Belle and Honey to close up the house.

They went through every room, meticulously locking every door and window. Finn and Joshua would have to wake up their butler in order to gain entrance into the house, assuming they returned at all this evening.

When they were done and ready to walk upstairs, Honey gave her a kiss on the cheek. "Sleep well. Don't worry about those Braydens. They know how to take care of themselves."

She nodded.

As they were about to climb the stairs, they heard riders pulling up to the front of the house. They rushed to the entry hall window and peered out. "It's Finn and Joshua," Honey muttered. "Oh, thank goodness. They're back."

Belle threw the bolt and opened the door.

Joshua strode in. "Finn's seeing to the horses. He'll be right along."

"What happened? Where were you all day?" She and Honey were both tossing questions at him. Then Holly came downstairs, fire iron in hand.

Joshua held up his hands in mock surrender. "Set down your sword, my fierce Valkyrie. It is only I, your meek and humble servant."

"Oh, for pity's sake." Holly shook her head and lowered her weapon. "Tell us what happened. I promise I won't hit you."

"We rode to London. Let me run upstairs and change out of these dusty clothes. Finn will likely want to do the same. We'll come back down and tell you what we've been doing. I'm thirsty. I could use a brandy."

"Of course," Honey said. "Are you hungry? There's leftover ham, potatoes, and leeks. I'll put a tray together for you and your brother."

Within the quarter-hour, the front door had been securely bolted again, and the five of them were seated around one of the small tables in the drawing room. Two lamps were lit, casting a golden glow around the room. Belle, Honey, and Holly were on the edge of their seats, waiting for the men to finish devouring their meal. They were gobbling down every morsel as though they hadn't seen food in years.

Holly was the first to prompt the men into talking. "Joshua said you rode to London."

Finn nodded. "We did." He washed down the ham with the last of his brandy and eased back in his chair. "We were gathering reinforcements."

Belle nibbled her lip. "What do you mean?"

"I had an audience with the Prince Regent today."

Honey blinked. "An audience…how did you manage this?"

Finn shrugged. "I have connections."

"Good connections," Joshua said, cutting off another slice of ham and barely cutting it up before packing it into his mouth while he continued to speak in muffled garbles.

"Lord Fortesque has overreached," Finn said, obviously repeating what his brother meant to tell them with his mouth full. "Had he restricted his blackmail to the lesser gentry and wealthy merchant class, no one would have cared. But he's been going after noble families as well, and word has reached Prinnie."

Belle was astounded. "You call him Prinnie?"

He nodded. "We are friends."

"The Prince Regent trusts my brother. I don't know why Finn's such a monumental arse at times." Joshua grinned. "But seriously, Finn is one of his most valued advisors."

"I am not. He ignores most of the advice I give him. But we are friends, as I said. It changes nothing. Even in private, we maintain formality. He'll be king once his father dies. He won't let any of us forget it, not that we ever would."

"He must like you if he's providing reinforcements." Belle shook her head. "What sort of reinforcements?"

"My army regiment," Joshua said. "They're up here now, camped just outside of Oxford. This is why we returned so late. First thing tomorrow morning, we're raiding every one of Fortesque's establishments and shutting them down. We're seizing his financial records. We're detaining his henchmen. He and his son will be escorted to London and held in our regimental headquarters until the Prince Regent authorizes their release."

Belle stared at Finn. "Can it be this simple? You make it sound as if his evil work can be easily put to an end."

Honey was staring at him, too. "What if he slips away?"

Joshua set down his knife and fork. "My soldiers and I will hunt him down. He's finished in Oxford. If he doesn't wish to hang, he'll agree to take everyone's secrets to the grave. If he refuses, I don't know that he'll make it out of London alive. In truth, I doubt he'll live to see next week. He's made too many powerful enemies. They'll get to him and kill him no matter how securely he is protected."

Finn reached out and placed his hand over Belle's, swallowing hers up in the warmth of his. "I know you think I can be ruthless, but I always prefer negotiation over physical force. However, Prinnie holds no such reservations. Fortesque has damaged several of his friends. While I may use force as a last resort, Prinnie and his friends will not. They are angry, and it is just as Joshua said—they will want him dead."

Joshua pushed aside his plate and continued Finn's thought. "And who will care what happens to Fortesque? He isn't in the House of Lords. He isn't one of the privileged few. His father was a marquess, but he isn't the eldest son. That he's referred to as Lord Fortesque is merely a courtesy in recognition of his father's rank."

"He's made too many enemies in Oxford," Finn said. "There'll be no outcry when he suddenly disappears. I'm sure the citizens will breathe a collective sigh of relief once they realize he's gone for good."

"What of his son?" Belle asked.

Finn caressed her hand. "Depends on how deeply he's been involved in his father's business. I suppose he'll try to make himself out as another of his father's victims, but we'll learn the truth once I have a look at their ledgers. Men lie all the time, but documents rarely lie." He rose and helped Belle to her feet. "Joshua and I have an early day tomorrow. We had better turn in."

"Of course." She placed her arm in his. "Oh, Finn. One more thing. We ladies spent the day in town today. Runyon was following us everywhere we went."

Finn frowned. "Homer and Mick reported the same to us a short while ago. I have them posted by the hedgerows to keep watch on the house this evening. They were also following you around Oxford today."

"They were?" Her eyes rounded in surprise.

Honey and Holly were equally surprised.

Finn nodded. "They're very good at what they do. Runyon has no finesse. He's a dolt, although I expect in this instance, Fortesque meant for him to be seen. He doesn't realize the anvil is dangling over his head now. He believes he's still in control of this town."

Belle kept Finn company as he returned the tray to the kitchen.

The others did a last pass through the house and retired upstairs.

Belle noticed Holly had left her fire iron at the foot of the stairs. "I'll take it up with me tonight and return it to her in the morning."

"I may not see you in the morning, love." Finn caressed her cheek. "Joshua and I will be off before dawn."

"I'm already missing you." She cast him a gentle smile. "Silly, isn't it?"

"Not at all. I'm feeling the same way."

"You are?" Belle cleared her throat. "Is it too much to ask...never mind. I doubt I'll be able to keep my hands off you. It is more important you are rested for tomorrow. Not to mention, it is thoroughly inappropriate and shocking."

He eyed her with astonishment. "Belle?"

"I shouldn't have said anything."

He was still eyeing her curiously as he escorted her upstairs. They paused at her door, the air noticeably charged between them. "I'll miss you like hell tonight," he said in a husky murmur, his breath warm against her ear. "But I dare not spend the night with you."

"No, of course not. I shouldn't have...are you angry with me for suggesting it?"

He grinned wryly. "Hell, no. I'm leaping for joy. You have no idea how badly I ache to hold your soft body in my arms, to touch you again, and feel you respond to me. But I need to keep my wits about me when dealing with Fortesque, and you, my love, will be too great a distraction. I'm too tired to be of much use anyway. I'd probably spend the hours snoring in your ear."

She placed her hand against his cheek, feeling the rough stubble of his day's growth of beard. "I wouldn't care. I love being in your arms. But you're right. You'll need to be very careful tomorrow. We'll have a lifetime to snore in each other's ears. I'm also very good at jabbing with my elbows. Honey always complains about that."

He smiled. "I look forward to the discomfort."

He kissed her deeply, then drew away and ran a hand through his hair. "Lord, you're tempting. Go in before I change my mind and do all sorts of indecent things to your delectable body."

She held up Holly's fire iron. "If you do change your mind, knock before you enter. I'm sleeping with this by my side and intend to hit first and ask questions later."

"Got it." He kissed her again. "See you tomorrow, love."

He waited for her to enter her chamber.

Belle heard his soft footsteps as he strode down the hall.

She closed her door but decided not to bolt it. If he wanted to come in, she had no intention of stopping him. Besides, the house was locked up tight, and the Bow Street runners were guarding it. Also, she had the fire iron for protection. "No one's getting in," she muttered, setting down Holly's weapon of choice beside her bed.

She sank onto the bed to kick off her shoes and remove her stockings, but she'd managed no more than removing her shoes before a dark shadow began to creep toward her. She grabbed the fire iron and attempted to scream, but her lungs were already seizing, and no sound came out. "He sent me to kill ye," Runyon said, his laughter soft and menacing.

She lunged forward to bang the iron against her footboard, hoping someone would hear, but he grabbed it out of her hand and tossed it aside. It landed with a muffled thud on the carpet, close enough for her to try to lunge for it again, if only she had the chance.

But her heart was beating so rapidly, she knew she was going to pass out soon. Now frantic, she reached for her table lamp to smash it against the wall.

"Oh, no ye don't." He caught her hand before she could throw it. "Ye're makin' it so easy for me." He mimicked her wheezes as she sank to her knees, her head spinning, and her body no longer in her control. "Can't breathe, lass? Isn't that a pity. I was going to strangle ye, but I think a pillow over the face will do just as well."

He must have assumed that her inability to breathe had already rendered her unable to move, for he turned away to cross the room and bolt the door. *Don't faint. Don't faint.* She forced herself to keep alert.

Breathe!

You're not a coward!

You can't let these villains win!

She reached for the fire iron within easy reach and used it to smash her lamp and then she began to pound it against her night table. Runyon immediately forgot about bolting the door and hurried back to her side to wrest the weapon out of her hand. She swung it with all her might and struck his knee.

"Ye'll die for this!" he screamed.

He grabbed her by the throat and began to press down on her airway. She tried to strike him again, but he'd pushed her to the floor and put his weight on her hand, so that the pain of it caused the iron to slip from her fingers.

Don't let me die. Please.

But she knew this was to be her fate.

She was going to die a horrible death.

She felt Runyon's fingers press on her throat, and despite her best efforts, she couldn't toss him off her.

Finn, I love you. I'm so sorry. I wasn't strong enough to fight him off.

She had almost given up when her bedroom door suddenly slammed open. She saw a blur of dark hair and a big body. *Finn!* Then Runyon was thrown off her, and the two men began to brawl. She heard one of them slam against her bureau. She heard their exchange of vicious blows as they punched and rolled into the hallway.

The noise had now brought everyone out of their bedchambers. Belle tried to take a deep breath. She would be safe now. Joshua had heard the scuffle and was running to help Finn subdue the villain. The two of them would take him down.

Yes, she was safe now. All she had to do was breathe.

But no air escaped from her lungs.

Nothing.

Honey was at her side, her voice calm.

She stared desperately at her sister. If she did not manage to breathe soon, even Honey would panic.

"Holly! Come in here and massage Belle's heart. Push down on it like this." Belle felt a pressure on her chest as her sister showed what was to be done and quickly allowed Holly to take over. "I'll be right back."

She watched Honey run down the servants' stairs and knew she had gone to grab a ginger tea or other healing tonic for her to drink.

She had to remain conscious to drink it, but her head was pounding, and her eyes were blurring. Her head was spinning wildly.

Concentrate on Finn.

He was fighting for her. She heard the thuds and grunts of a horrifically brutal struggle and couldn't fail him.

In the next moment, she heard a crash and a scream, then a thud as something hit the entry hall's marble floor below. "That's one big, ugly bastard," Joshua said, breathing heavily as he hurried into her bedchamber.

Holly looked up at him in alarm. "What about Finn?"

"He's checking to see if Runyon's dead." He knelt beside them. "I'll take some footmen with me now to make sure our Bow Street runners are unharmed. I don't know how he got around them. Wait, what's wrong with Belle?"

"Finn, thank goodness," Holly cried, looking beyond Joshua as Finn rushed in. "She...I can't..."

Finn knelt beside Belle. "I'll take over. Belle, love. Can you hear me?"

She blinked in response.

"Good, love. Can you take a breath?" His voice was remarkably calm, and it helped to calm her as well, but her breaths still would not come.

Holly was growing agitated. "She can't. She's trying to, but it isn't helping. Oh, Finn!"

He drew Belle into his arms. "I'm going to breathe into your mouth now." He bent over her, and she felt the press of his mouth on hers and the sudden force of his breath rushing into her. He did it several times, alternating between breathing air into her lungs and massaging her heart until she felt herself begin to wheeze again.

He held her hand and continued to encourage her with his soothing words. The deep, resonant sound of his voice calmed her so that she was starting to get air. He helped her to sit up and had his arms wrapped around her when Honey returned with the ginger tea a short while later.

Her hands shook as she drank it slowly.

Everyone but Joshua now stood around her, including her parents, who looked as though they were about to faint. The room was in shambles. There was broken glass and broken furniture everywhere. "Runyon?" she asked in a croaking voice.

"He tried to push Finn and Joshua over the railing, but he missed and fell over it instead," Dahlia replied. "He landed on his head on the marble. It's a mess. His head is smashed open like a melon tossed off the roof of a building. There's blood splattered everywhere. *His* blood."

"Dahlia! Stop!" Heather frowned at her. "You're awfully lurid. You'll make Belle ill."

Finn kissed the top of her head. "Are you all right?"

She nodded. "I can breathe. I'll be fine in a few minutes."

He eased her out of his arms and gave her over to Honey and Holly. "Take care of her. Fortesque must have been warned of our raids. We have to get to him before he slips away."

Belle's eyes rounded in alarm. "You can't go alone!"

"No, love. I have an entire regiment with me. Joshua's men." He kissed her on the brow. "Get some rest. I'll see you in the morning. And about those wedding plans. Scrap them."

"You don't want to marry me?" She held back the tears threatening to fall. "I understand. I ought to have known."

"Hen's teeth, you are the most dense girl I've ever met. I don't want to marry you in a week's time. You and I are getting married tomorrow. I'm not spending another night apart from you. What do you say, Belle? Will you marry me tomorrow?"

CHAPTER FIFTEEN

F INN STOOD FACING Belle beside the altar in the chapel at Magdalen
College the following afternoon. He probably looked like a love-
smitten fool, which is what he was, and he did not care who knew it.
The special license he'd obtained permitted him to marry this
beautiful, tawny-haired angel anywhere and at any time of day, a
convenient circumstance because he'd meant what he said yesterday.
He was not going to spend another night apart from her.

The minister was eyeing them skeptically, as though they were the
most bedraggled wedding party he had ever beheld. Finn's right eye
was blackened, and his lip was cut. Joshua looked no better, for his left
eye was blackened, and he had a cut on his cheek that would leave a
permanent scar. He and his brother looked like hell warmed over
because they'd spent last night and the better part of this morning
rounding up Lord Fortesque, his son, and their confederates.

The task was now done, and Joshua's regiment had matters well
under control.

He smiled at Belle. "Ready, love?"

She looked incredibly beautiful, even though her throat was
bruised where Runyon had pressed down on it while attempting to
choke her. Finn suppressed a shudder. The bastard could have crushed
her windpipe, and would have if Finn had taken a second longer to
reach her.

She nodded. "Yes, I'm ready. But I still don't understand why you'd settle for a wife with bad lungs."

He knew she spoke in jest, and he liked that she felt comfortable enough to tease him. More importantly, she felt comfortable enough to make herself the butt of her teasing. Finally, after all these years of being beaten down even by those who loved her, she'd gained confidence in herself.

After all they'd been through this week, he did not think anything could ever separate them again. So, when they exchanged their marriage vows, pledged their hearts and bodies to each other for the rest of their lives, it meant something quite profound to both of them.

"Forever, my love," he whispered.

"Yes, Finn. Forever. I will love you always."

It felt like ages ago they'd read *The Book of Love*, but Finn remembered every word. The initial attraction, the lure of the senses. The bonds they would forge over time. Belle grew more beautiful in his eyes with each passing day. Each passing hour. Each passing minute.

He, on the other hand, looked like something the cat dragged in. But she was still smiling up at him with stars in her eyes.

Joshua, who was standing beside them at the altar, kissed her on the cheek when the ceremony ended, and they'd been declared husband and wife. "Belle, I still don't understand why you'd settle for a monumental arse like my brother."

Finn was happy. He knew Joshua was happy for him. The two of them were grinning at each other like a pair of hyenas. But being the older brother, Finn could not let the comment go unanswered. "And you look like my arse. In fact, I think my arse is far better looking than your ugly face."

Usually, they'd proceed to punch each other playfully, but they were both in too much pain to risk it. Instead, they exchanged brotherly hugs, glad to be alive and knowing Belle and her family would now be safe.

Joshua stepped back, laughing. "Gad, what is this world coming to?

You and Tynan now married, and despite being idiots, you've managed to choose beautiful, intelligent wives. However, I'm not sure what it says about their lapse in good sense."

Finn rolled his eyes. "It means there's hope even for undeserving dolts like you and Ronan."

"In good time, don't rush us. We're not looking for any permanent arrangements yet. Perhaps when we're as old and ugly as you and Ty."

Finn gazed down at his swollen hand before returning his attention to Joshua. "I'd punch you, but it would probably hurt me more than you."

"Save your strength for tonight and your lovely bride. After the wedding breakfast, which is more like a wedding supper, I intend to spend the night stumbling from tavern to tavern with the officers in my regiment. No young lovely will leg-shackle me before I'm good and ready. I still have years of fun left in me."

"Josh, shut up already. If marriage is so abhorrent to you, then why are you constantly talking about it?"

Joshua grumbled and cast him a frown. "I'm not talking about it."

Finn chuckled. "Right."

Joshua stepped back as Belle's sister, cousins, and parents began to cluster around them. Finn took Belle's hand and held it very lightly. His hand was sore and swollen, and hers was wrapped in a bandage because Runyan had ground his weight down on it and sprained her wrist.

Fortunately, they would all recover, even the Bow Street runners who had managed to subdue six of Fortesque's henchmen when they came to the Farthingale home along with Runyon last night.

Finn suppressed a shudder, very well aware it was a miracle everyone was safe.

Belle was still looking at him starry-eyed. "Finn, I have something important to confess to you."

"Oh, lord. You're not about to confess another secret, are you?"

"Yes, I'm afraid so." She nibbled her lip, one of the luscious lips he'd be tasting and nibbling later this evening.

He groaned. "What is it, love?"

"It's about my formulas. I told you they were in a code that Fortesque would never be able to break."

"I remember."

"Well, the truth is, he'd never be able to break the codes because they are gibberish."

He shook his head, confused. "So where are the real codes kept?"

"They don't exist. The formulas are all in my head. I've memorized all seventy of them. Honey and I decided never to write them down. I'm sorry I lied to you about that. I wanted to tell you the truth but was afraid someone would overhear us in the shop and tell Fortesque it was all rubbish."

"Hen's teeth," he said softly.

"However, we do enjoy playing with ciphers. And now that we're older and wiser, we understand the need to actually jot everything down so these formulas, whether in code or not, can be passed on to the next generation of Farthingales...or Brayden-Farthingales."

Finn gazed at her in horror. "Belle, is nothing at all written down? What were you thinking? Your family business is built on your nose. Without those formulas...it would be worthless. What if something had happened to you?"

"As it nearly did last night?" She nodded. "As I said, Honey and I understand that now. We meant to write them all down shortly before the trouble began. Then our father started acting strangely, and we put it off. But not a moment longer, I promise. This will be Honey's and my new project. Of course, we'll need to retain a business advisor. Preferably one who is tall, dark, and handsome. With gorgeous grayish-green eyes, if possible. Do you have any such man to recommend?" She kissed him. "I would be willing to exchange bedroom favors for his advice."

He laughed. "I think I know one who would be obsessively devoted to you."

"Thank you, Finn. We'd appreciate your help in getting our shops and products in good order." She cleared her throat. "However, I'm worried about Honey. We may have managed to keep our secret quiet, but she is honorable to a fault. She will never marry a man under false pretenses. I don't want her to miss out on love because of our circumstances. And she's so proud. Too proud. She'd rather die a spinster than deceive the man she wishes to marry."

Finn nodded. "She's beautiful and clever. Once everything quiets down, perhaps she'll find someone she will trust enough to share her secret. He's out there, I promise. She will find a good man who will love her enough that this heinous word, *illegitimate*, won't matter."

"I hope so. But I'm not leaving anything to chance. I've given her *The Book of Love*."

He laughed and shook his head. "Belle, my love. Don't you realize the book holds no magic?"

"Yes, it does. How can you deny it? It brought you to me, and by some miracle, you fell in love with me."

"It was easy to fall in love with you. It didn't take a miracle, only a cup of spilled tea."

She sighed, knowing he still remained doubtful. "We found each other the moment I was given the book. That is nothing short of a miracle."

He kissed her on the lips. "Yes, I suppose it is."

Later that evening, when they were once again alone, this time in a magnificent suite at Oxford's fanciest inn, Finn showed her just how magical their lives as husband and wife would be together.

Belle now understood what it meant when couples *coupled*. But it had a far greater meaning when two people in love shared their bodies with each other, as she and Finn had done twice this evening. As the light of dawn filtered in through the sheer curtains to mark the start of a glorious new day, Finn drew her up against his big, warm body.

"Are you awake, Belle?"

She nodded against her pillow. "Yes, did I accidentally jab you with my elbow?"

"No, love. It was your breasts that woke me."

"My breasts?" She laughed sleepily. "They are nowhere near you. In fact, I am turned away from you, my back to your front."

"And that is the problem. I've been missing them terribly."

Smiling, she turned to face him, pressing herself to his chest as she snuggled in the circle of his arms. "Better?"

"Lord, yes." He cupped her breast and then bent his head to take one taut peak into his mouth. She sighed as he gently teased it, suckled it, and flicked his tongue over it with a hot sensuality she was helpless to resist.

"Finn," she said in an aching whisper, twining her fingers in his hair.

"I know, love. I can't get enough of you. I'm sorry if I woke you."

"Heavens, I'm not sorry in the least."

"Thank goodness."

He settled between her legs, and as the birds outside their window chirped to welcome the sunrise, and the scent of dew-tinged roses swept into their room on the gentle breeze, Belle took him into her body and moved with him as he sought his pleasure. True to Finn's protective and valiant nature, he took care of her first, but she hoped they'd reach their heights together.

She clasped his shoulders as his manhood thrust into her, met his lips, and returned his kisses as hungrily as he sought hers. She was so aroused and on fire that she was ready and did not hold back, meeting him thrust for thrust, and knowing the moment when he met his release.

"I love you," she whispered and soared with him.

When the waves of their passion finally subsided, he eased out of her, but she stopped him before he could roll off her. "Not yet, Finn. Please."

"Love, I don't want to crush you."

"You're not. You won't. I love the way we feel together."

He kissed her on the lips. "So do I."

"I can hear your heart pounding." He tried to ease his weight onto his elbows, but she stopped him again. "In a moment, Finn. I crave the warmth of your body a moment longer. Let me revel in the afterglow."

He arched an eyebrow and grinned. "Reveling, is it? You will make my head swell to insufferable proportions."

She closed her eyes and inhaled lightly.

When she inhaled again, he growled in concern and shifted off her, rolling her gently so that she now lay atop him. "Belle, open your eyes. Are you all right?"

She nodded and took another deep breath.

He caressed her cheek. "What are you doing?"

She opened her eyes and smiled at him. "Isn't it obvious? I'm trying to memorize the scent of your male heat. How else am I to capture the scent of love?"

"The scent of...? No! Don't you dare!" But he was laughing and caressing her hair. He cupped her face in his hands and kissed her on the mouth. "There is nothing remotely enticing about a sweaty, spent man. Don't you dare think to bottle my...spillage."

"Ugh!" She sank back against her pillows and wrinkled her nose, but she settled back atop him a moment later, her eyes bright and her brain working at a fervent speed. "But it is an intriguing idea, isn't it? The notion that love can be bottled. Can you imagine the frenzy if I concocted a love potion?"

"No, don't even think about it. A book on love is bad enough. See where it got us?"

"Gloriously happy and making wild, passionate love to each other throughout our first night of wedded bliss. What is so bad about that?"

"Nothing, but that isn't the point."

"Then what is the point?"

He growled low in his throat. "Hell if I know. Come here, my love."

"I am right here, lying atop you. Haven't you noticed?"

"Indeed, I have. But I'm not inside you. I'm missing your body again."

"What an amazing coincidence, I happen to be aching for yours." She kissed him on his shoulders that were hard and muscled as though sculpted out of stone.

"I love you, Belle."

"I love you, too," she said and surrendered to the magic of the moment...but surely such a splendid thing could be bottled, couldn't it?

Finn growled again. "I can hear you thinking."

"Well, what are you going to do about it?"

He proceeded to use his lips and tongue to ready her so that she was carried over the edge to mindless pleasure as soon as he entered her. Perhaps Finn was right, this was their heat, their scent, their love to share only with each other.

Afterward, she rested in his arms, knowing deep contentment. She wanted her sister to find this same happiness. Honey was now so resistant, believing herself inferior. Belle understood this better than anyone since she'd lived with this feeling all her life until Finn came along and captured her heart.

But who would save Honey?

EPILOGUE

London, two weeks later

"**Y**OU JUST HAPPENED to look at my calendar?" Finn was livid. He shut the door to his office so his clerks would not hear the berating lecture he was about to give his mother. He would not mince words. Lady Miranda Grayfell was no meek flower, and she had to be stopped before she unwittingly trampled over his and Belle's privacy.

How was it possible for this meddlesome woman to stop by his office in the ten minutes he'd stepped out, rummage through his desk drawers, and happen to stumble upon his calendar and the notation *Appointment with Lady X* marked in four consecutive days on it?

"Who is Lady X? How can you do this, Finn? You're a married man now! I will not have my son cavorting with—"

"I am not a three-year-old you can spank if he misbehaves." He frowned back at her, knowing he had to regain control of the situation from his strong-willed mother. Hah! Strong-willed was an understatement. Lady Miranda was a warrior of a woman, with blazing red hair. Henna, of course. But she'd crush his skull with a battle mace if he ever dared mention it.

"Such women will give you the pox. Is this what you want, Finn? To die childless and diseased before you ever reach the age of thirty? And what if you give this awful disease to poor, sweet, trusting Belle?"

Gad, could this get any worse?

"Out," he ordered, taking her by the elbow. "If you interfere in my marriage, so help me, I will evict you from my townhouse."

She gasped. "You don't mean that. You'd never be so cruel to me."

Of course, he wouldn't.

He loved her. "Don't put it to the test."

When tears began to form in her eyes, he groaned and gave in the slightest bit. "I am not an idiot. Why must you always jump to the worst conclusion? That notation is a month old and not at all what you believe it is."

"You must confess this to Belle and beg her forgiveness."

"Confess what?" Belle asked, walking into his office at that very moment. "I was nearby shopping and thought I'd stop in to see you, my love. What must I forgive you for?"

He smiled and came around his desk to kiss her. "My mother and I were talking about a matter that is extremely delicate and has to do with a financial situation."

"Financial! Hah!" His mother reached into her reticule, and for a moment, Finn wondered whether she was going to pull out a pistol and shoot him. Thankfully, she withdrew her lace handkerchief instead.

"Yes, financial. This is what I do, as you well know. It has nothing to do with my lustful urges."

"Finn! Watch your language. I'm your mother." She glanced in panic at Belle. "And your *wife* is here."

"Thank you for alerting me to that fact," he said dryly. "How are you, my love? Enjoying your day?"

Belle nodded. "Yes, very much. Especially now that I'm here with you. But I only stopped in to give you a kiss. My sister and cousins are waiting downstairs. We're done shopping for the day and thought we'd stop for tea and cakes at one of the local shops before returning to Uncle John and Aunt Sophie's. Care to join us? And you, too, Lady Miranda. We'd love to have you with us."

His mother muffled a sob by placing her handkerchief to her

mouth.

Belle frowned. "Oh, dear. Is something wrong?"

Finn sighed and handed her the calendar. "She's caught me, Belle. And now I must confess my love for Lady X."

"Finn!" His mother looked at him as though he'd just lost his mind.

"No, Mother. You're right. Belle must be told. I'm sorry, Belle. She's the only one for me. The only woman I shall ever love."

"I have it on good authority that Lady X loves you to distraction, too. She will never love anyone but you." She kissed him on the cheek. "Now, you must stop being so cruel and tell your mother."

"Tell me what?" His mother still looked dazed.

Belle, being too softhearted, gave his mother a hug. "Oh, Miranda! I'm Lady X. How can you think Finn would ever be unfaithful to me? There's no one else. I came to him seeking help with my family's business, and he jestingly put me into his calendar as his mysterious Lady X. He's the most wonderful, noble, honorable man in all of England. You've raised a magnificent son."

Miranda sank into a chair, shaking her head with relief. "I am obviously losing my touch. But watching my boys turn into men has been quite difficult for me. Now Ronan and Joshua are determined to sow their wild oats, and I was afraid they'd led Finn astray with their behavior."

Belle frowned at Finn. "Have your brothers been misbehaving?"

He shrugged. "I don't know. Honest, Belle. I haven't been paying attention to them. My thoughts have all been on you."

"Oh, thank you, my love."

He turned to his mother. "What's been going on?"

"I'm not sure. But I overheard them talking. Snippets, really. Unfortunately, I couldn't catch most of what they were saying. But I think Ronan is secretly running around with a betrothed young lady. That boy is shameful!"

Finn arched an eyebrow. "I'd say the young lady is the one behaving shamefully. She's the one breaking her vows before she's even married. What about Joshua? What has he done to overset you?"

"I think he's seeing an older woman. A shameless hussy of a widow. No doubt her husband left her wealthy, and now she's set herself up in a tawdry lair—"

"Also known as a fashionable townhouse," Finn said, unable to resist laughing.

"It isn't funny, Finn. You mustn't mock me. Your brothers need to spend more time in church. I despair of saving them from the path of ruin." She sighed and turned to Belle. "I pray you have biddable daughters. Sons will make your hair turn gray prematurely. Fortunately, mine has stayed naturally red."

Finn made a choking sound, then coughed and turned away to stare out his window at the flowing waters of the Thames.

"See, boys are the very devil. But daughters are loving and sweet. I do adore you and your sister. Too bad Honey has shown no interest in my boys. And now she's leaving town for Lord Wycke's country party. Well, I hope she has a nice time. But do warn her about that handsome cad. He can be quite persuasive when he turns on the charm, and I don't believe he is seriously looking for a bride."

"Oh, I see."

Miranda nodded. "Although he would be quite a catch. Handsome, wealthy, and an earl. What is there not to love?"

Belle exchanged a smile with Finn. "I'll warn my sister about that handsome beast." She invited Lady Miranda to join her and her family for tea again, but she declined, hugged her fiercely, and hurried off in the same whirl of wind that had brought her in.

"Finn..."

He took her in his arms and kissed her on the brow. "Yes, love?"

"Do you think the Earl of Wycke is the man meant to fall in love with Honey? His name has been coming up with hers all day. It's odd, isn't it?"

"I don't know. But you've given her that *Book of Love*, so who knows what will happen?"

Belle nodded. "After that terrible ordeal in Oxford, our horrible secret…"

"I know, love. I wish there was something I could do to fix the cruel and undeserved taint."

"There's nothing any of us can do. It happened. Honey and I will have to live with the knowledge for the rest of our lives. But I'm worried about her."

"She's strong and smart."

"But she takes things very much to heart. We had originally accepted Lord Wycke's invitation. Honey wrote back to him and politely bowed out. Do you think she made a mistake in doing so? Shall I convince her to go? No one else but Lord Wycke knows she has declined."

Finn's arms tightened around her, and he kissed her on the cheek. "Don't meddle, love. If that book is magical, as you seem to think it is, then let it do whatever it's meant to do."

"But Farthingales always meddle. What if I'm meant to convince her? What if I ruin her chance at happiness by staying quiet?"

He groaned. "Fine, do what your heart tells you to do."

She kissed him again, wanting very badly to remain in his arms. "I had better go. Everyone's waiting for me. I love you, Finn."

He nuzzled her neck. "I'll see you in your boudoir later this evening…Lady X."

Also by Meara Platt

FARTHINGALE SERIES
My Fair Lily
The Duke I'm Going To Marry
Rules For Reforming A Rake
A Midsummer's Kiss
The Viscount's Rose
Earl Of Hearts
If You Wished For Me
Never Dare A Duke
Capturing The Heart Of A
Cameron

THE BOOK OF LOVE SERIES
The Look of Love
The Touch of Love
The Taste of Love
The Song of Love
The Scent of Love
The Kiss of Love
The Hope of Love

THE BRAYDENS
A Match Made In Duty
Earl of Westcliff
Fortune's Dragon
Earl of Kinross
Pearls of Fire

DARK GARDENS SERIES
Garden of Shadows
Garden of Light
Garden of Dragons
Garden of Destiny

De WOLFE "ANGELS"
SERIES
Nobody's Angel
Kiss An Angel
Bhrodi's Angel

About the Author

Meara Platt is a USA Today bestselling author and an award winning, Amazon UK All-star. Her favorite place in all the world is England's Lake District, which may not come as a surprise since many of her stories are set in that idyllic landscape, including her award-winning paranormal romance Dark Gardens series. If you'd like to learn more about the ancient Fae prophecy that is about to unfold in the Dark Gardens series, as well as Meara's lighthearted, international bestselling Regency romances in the Farthingale series, Book of Love series, and the Braydens series, please visit Meara's website at www.mearaplatt.com.

Made in the USA
Columbia, SC
05 June 2025

59007134R00109